THE WOODS ARE ALWAYS WATCHING

STEPHANIE PERKINS

MACMILLAN

First published in the US 2021 by Dutton Books,
an imprint of Penguin Random House LLC

First published in the UK 2021 by Macmillan Children's Books
an imprint of Pan Macmillan
The Smithson, 6 Briset Street, London EC1M 5NR
EU representative: Macmillan Publishers Ireland Ltd, 1st Floor,
The Liffey Trust Centre, 117–126 Sheriff Street Upper
Dublin 1, D01 YC43
Associated companies throughout the world
www.panmacmillan.com

ISBN 978-1-5098-6032-6

3 5 7 9 8 6 4 2

A CIP catalogue record for this book is available from the British Library.

Designed by Anna-Booth
Printed and bound by CPI Group (UK) Ltd, Croydon CR0 4YY

For Jarrod, best friend & true love

TOGETHER

NEENA CUT THE engine, and the speakers went silent. Mid-lyric. The trail was straight ahead, but her gaze could only follow it to its first bend. The overhanging forest, a drab and washed-out green that presaged the end of summer, obscured the rest of the path.

"How many days do you think we'll last?" she asked.

"How many hours," Josie said.

"If I die out there? I'd be honored if you ate my body."

"I would *never* let a bear get to your body first."

"Oh my God." Incredulity tainted Neena's laughter. "Would you please stop it with the bears?"

"Only if you promise not to mention their existence for the next seventy-two hours."

"I didn't! *You* brought them up. Again."

Josie shuddered, darkening. "I'm serious. I don't know if I can do this."

"Just think of them as big Winnie-the-Poohs."

"Shut your hole."

"Paddingtons. Baloos. Fozzies."

It was a joke—it was always a joke—but Josie jerked open the passenger-side door and got out. It slammed shut behind her. Neena grabbed her phone off the charger and followed her best friend into the parking lot.

"Berenstains," she said, digging in. Neena always dug in.

Her hiking boots crunched against the wet gravel. The rain had just stopped. In these mountains, it rained most afternoons during the summer—violent downpours in the early season, irksome drizzles in the late—but cleared quickly. It was the third week of August. The Little South Chickadee River burbled and sang nearby. Insects hummed and clicked their wings. The lazy breeze smelled of sun-warmed pine.

Josie pivoted with sudden interest. "Ooh, did you ever have a thing for Brother Bear? I mean, before you realized they were über-Christian hillbillies."

"What are you talking about?" Neena asked, confused.

"Brother Bear. With the red shirt and blue pants."

"I know who Brother Bear is. The Berenstain Bears were Christian?"

"There were numerous books with the word 'God' in the title."

"Huh," Neena said. "I guess my parents didn't check those out from the library." She popped the Subaru's hatch. Everyone in Asheville drove a Subaru, the preferred mode of transportation for modern hippies and outdoorsmen, among which the girls were neither. Neena's parents had purchased the Impreza because it had a high safety rating. Their backpacks crowded its hatch like monstrous, bloated caterpillars. Very hungry caterpillars. Neena realized her thoughts might be stuck on picture books.

She moaned. "I don't wanna."

Josie copied Neena's moan. "I don't wanna, either."

The packs didn't budge, refusing to help. These were not their school backpacks, retired from service and recently replaced by more stylish backpacks for college. Josie's brother and his girlfriend had loaned them a pair of backpacking packs: a boggling assemblage of padded straps, hip belts, bungee cords, mesh pockets, and bulging compartments. Neena prickled with renewed trepidation. Not only were these packs borrowed, but so was the equipment inside them. Even her boots—an outmoded pair, heavy and ugly—were borrowed from Josie's mom, who wore the same size.

Unfortunately, they had no one to blame but themselves. The trip had been concocted only two days ago during their morning shift at Kmart, a pre-Amazon relic where customers often exclaimed in astonishment, "I thought you went under years ago!"

Alas. The chain clung on for its meager life. Their particular location had a whopping 1.5-star rating on Yelp. Its shelves were largely empty and in permanent disarray. Clothing hung askew on broken racks, dented cans lingered past expiration dates, sports equipment was shellacked in off-putting colors, and the book selection was a smattering of religious overstock and failed themed-mystery series. *The Thanksgiving Murders. The Body on the Badminton Court. 'Til Death Do Us Sudoku.* The store looked like a former roommate had never returned to pick up the last of his boxes.

That Saturday shift had been Neena's last. In one week, she would be moving to California for college. Josie was staying in North Carolina.

"We should do something," Neena had said.

"We are doing something," Josie had replied flatly. "We're restocking the shampoo aisle."

"Something significant. Something just the two of us."

"It's always just the two of us."

Though her gaze had remained detached, Josie's eyelids twitched at her own slip. It wouldn't *always* be just the two of them. The impending separation pressed against them like a loaded shotgun.

Josie was acting glum and bitter, as she had been all summer. Neena longed for the old Josie, who was lively and game. She needed the old Josie. She'd tried again. "Something big, I mean. Maybe we could drive to Dollywood."

"Roller coasters give you migraines."

"We could go camping. Like Galen and Kyle."

"We hate Galen and Kyle," Josie had said. They hated everybody; it was one of the things that had sealed their friendship. But their teenage redneck coworkers were particularly loathsome. They spat watery brown dip onto the break-room floor, ignored calls to the registers for backup, and viewed feminism as a threat to their masculinity. "And we don't know shit about camping. Nature is for . . . other people."

Their classmates had all taken advantage of the mountain lifestyle. They had always been off tubing and kayaking down the French Broad River, hiking and camping along the Blue Ridge Parkway. A lot of beer, weed, and sex had been involved. It was a local rite of passage. Neena and Josie had never been interested in any of that, excepting the sex. But, regrettably, neither of them had ever had a boyfriend.

"Yeah," Neena had said, "but if they can do it, so can we. Didn't you used to go camping with your family?"

"When I was a kid. And my dad and Win did all the work."

Josie's father had died when she was in the eighth grade. Win was Winston, Josie's older brother. It was unnecessary to point out that Neena had never been camping. Everyone in her family was strictly an indoor type. Despite this, Neena unexpectedly latched onto the idea. "Okay, but Win goes all the time. We could borrow his gear." Her reasoning crumbled into pleading. "I mean, haven't you ever wondered if *maybe* we missed out on a vital high school experience?"

Josie had snorted with disdain. But she'd stopped restocking.

"Soon I won't even have the option to do things like this any-more," Neena had said. "Not in the city. This is my last chance."

Neena wasn't sure why Josie had eventually come around. Maybe because Neena had continued to monologue, hyping the excursion with notions of enlightenment. Being in the woods would be free-ing! A technology detox! A chance to commune with Mother Earth, Mother Nature . . . whatever her name was! But by the time Neena had clocked out for the last time from the not-so-superstore, Josie had switched enough shifts so they could do it. Of course, they still needed permission. They had wanted to leave the next morning, but it took longer than that just to convince Neena's parents.

I won't see Josie again until Thanksgiving.

You will not see us until Thanksgiving, either.

I'm an adult.

You are eighteen.

I've never gotten into trouble.

You have never been given the chance, because we keep you safe.

Neena's father had relented first. Maybe it was because he'd spent more time with Josie, driving the girls around before Neena had gotten her license. Fixing them hot dogs and jhal muri after school. Watching every season of endless sitcoms with them. As the primary witness to their friendship, perhaps he held deeper compassion for their situation.

Our daughter is right, Baba had said, wearily rubbing his brow. Neena had been surprised to be right. *She is responsible and trustwor-thy. She has earned this.*

The trip would last three days, and the girls had decided to go backpacking, which, best they could tell, meant "hiking with camp-ing." Camping-only sounded boring. Josie's brother had helped them select a trail, and, ever the diligent students, they crammed their research—reading articles, watching videos, scouring message boards. They'd organized an itinerary and printed out copies for their families. They'd downloaded trail-map apps onto their phones and marked the waypoints.

But Neena's parents still wouldn't give their final blessing until the girls proved they could use the equipment. Earlier that morning, all three parents had stood in Josie's overgrown backyard, scrutinizing them as they pitched the tent, lit the stove, and filtered water under Win's tutelage. The girls were unskilled and clumsy, and everyone had a good chuckle at their expense, but they'd passed the test. They excelled at passing tests.

And now they were here. And so were their enormous backpacks.

"Do you remember how we're supposed to put them on?" Neena tried to recall Win's backpack demonstration, but it blurred with all his other demonstrations and instructions.

Josie frowned. "Something to do with the knees. Or a knee? There's definitely some kind of knee-to-shoulder transfer. I think."

They glanced at each other. The absurdity of not even knowing the very first step broke them into nervous, hysterical giggles.

Neena reached for her pack. "Here goes nothing."

Literally nothing went. The pack was leaden.

"Well," Neena said. "Shit."

They cracked up harder. Using all four hands, together the girls scooted and grunted the behemoth forward, until Neena's pack was half on the car, half off. They were in tears from laughing.

"Was it this heavy when we put it in here?" Josie asked.

"I think it birthed a baby hippopotamus." Neena unzipped the pack's hip-belt pocket and squeezed her phone inside. Service didn't exist out here, but they'd packed a charging device so they could still use their cameras and GPS. They had been surprised to learn that

GPS would still work. Win had explained that it connected to satellites, not cell towers. The girls' last texts had been sent from a remote highway on the outskirts of Canton, just past a guzzling old paper mill. The cell signals had vanished soon after. Their families did not expect to hear from them again until they returned.

Josie pointed at the pack's straps, which were dangling above the ground. "Can you get underneath, maybe? Could you try to slip those on?"

Neena glanced around to ensure that no one else was watching. But it was a Monday, a weekday, and this wasn't a popular trail. Another Subaru was parked at the east end of the lot, because of course it was, and two pickups were parked at the west. The rest of the lot was empty—the weekend hikers and campers had already gone home.

Crouching below her target, Neena turtled it onto her body. Her arms threaded through the straps, her right foot took a labored step, the pack dislodged . . . and then slowly, steadily pushed her straight into the ground.

Josie lost her mind. She buckled over again, clutching her abdomen.

The crush was so alarming that Neena laughed, too, out of shock. Her clothes sponged up the sodden earth. "I don't recommend this method."

"I've never seen actual slow motion in real life."

"Hey. Help a gal out?"

It took a full minute for Josie to roll Neena over, and then for Neena to rock back and forth to gain some momentum. But, finally, Neena heaved upward.

Josie grabbed Neena's flailing hands. Their matching rings caught in the sunlight, glittering like miniature galaxies. The rings were all stone, no metal—carved ultramarine with clouds of white calcite and flecks of gold pyrite. Last winter, the girls had purchased them at a mineral shop downtown because the sign had claimed that lapis lazuli was a symbol of friendship. The rings had adorned their right index fingers ever since.

Josie lifted Neena to her feet and didn't let go until Neena was steady. "You look fantastic," she said. "Like you're ready to summit Everest."

Dampness muddied Neena's clothing. Gravel stuck to her cheek. "Ugh, this thing weighs a thousand pounds. People do this for fun?" She brushed the grit from her jeans.

Josie was wearing jeans, too, to shield her legs from ticks, which were abundant here and carried Lyme disease. "Cotton kills," Win had warned, a favorite refrain of the outdoor community. But he wasn't talking about protection from bloodsucking arachnids. Cotton was dangerous because it absorbed moisture and lacked insulation. Unfortunately, their choices were either jeans or leggings—the girls didn't own any other types of pants—and leggings weren't warm enough. Because he'd also said it got cold out here at night, even in August, even though they were only fifty-five minutes from home.

Neena snapped her hip belt together. "Your turn."

Josie wished it weren't. She had only agreed to this trip because Neena had begged, and because their days together were at an end. The trip almost hadn't even happened. Josie had allowed Neena to believe that Neena's parents were the holdup, but the truth was that Josie's mother had been equally resistant. She'd only relented after Win had intervened. Josie had overheard his muffled appeal from the other side of her bedroom wall. *Her best friend is moving away. Just let her have this.* It stung to hear her circumstances described so plainly.

Everything about this summer stung because Neena was leaving, and Josie was staying.

Neena was going to attend the University of Southern California, and Josie was going to attend the University of North Carolina Asheville.

Neena was going to live in a dormitory, and Josie was going to keep living at home with her mother.

Neena was going to have new friends and new experiences, and Josie was going to be surrounded by all the same people and places.

It wasn't that Josie didn't love their hometown. Asheville was beautiful and open-minded and had multiple concert venues, independent cinemas, and organic farmers' markets. It had Arts and Crafts neighborhoods and an Art Deco downtown. It had character and history and integrity. But it was also small—the kind of city that adults chose to live in *after* they'd explored the rest of the world. Neena was about to see the world without her. Josie was about to become a human Kmart. Abandoned and forgotten, but still here.

"Sorry I can't help you anymore," Neena said, shuffling toward her.

Josie startled. "What?"

"With your pack. We should have moved yours, too, before I put on mine."

Sometimes Josie believed, sincerely, that Neena could read her mind. She was glad this wasn't one of the occasions. Putting on a show of false enthusiasm and roaring with exaggerated strength, Josie hefted her pack to the edge of the hatch.

Neena blinked at her. Mystified. "How'd you do that?"

"You've got the food. I've got the tent. The food weighs more."

"Fuck that. You're taking the food tomorrow."

Josie grinned, for real. "After we've already eaten some? No problem."

"You devious, devious wench."

"That was the deal. You got the lady backpack, so you got the extra pounds." Josie shoved her pack into an upright position. It took several attempts before it stayed.

"I got the lady backpack because I'm shorter than you. And I still think the lady backpack should necessitate fewer pounds."

"The lady backpack distributes the weight more evenly across the lady's body."

Neena waddled in a circle. Her hands were posed like she was modeling. "Now, tell me. Is it this luscious shade of purple that makes it a lady backpack?"

"Luscious lavender."

"*Ladies in Lavender* . . . wasn't that a movie with Judi Dench?"

"And Maggie Smith. They nurse a sexy, young violinist back to health."

"When we're old," Neena said, "I want us to be surrounded by sexy, young violinists."

"I'd settle for us just being Dames," Josie said. Her pack was navy blue and stained from years of rugged use. Win had started solo backpacking after their father's death. Their father had loved the outdoors, and, in his grief, her brother had found refuge there. He'd been seventeen then, only a few months younger than Josie was now. It was a surprising realization. Now Win was twenty-two, but it seemed like he'd been an adult forever.

Meegan, owner of the lavender pack, had only taken up backpacking when she and Win started dating. Josie hoped she would never stoop to something like that. But if a guy ever showed any interest in her, maybe she'd take up a dumb hobby to impress him, too.

"Obviously we'll be Dames," Neena said.

Josie loved talking with Neena like this. Like their future was certain. Like they would always be friends. She backed up neatly into her upright pack, slipped the straps over her shoulders, snapped it all together, and stood.

"Aw," Neena said. "That's not fair."

Compared to Neena, Josie was tall. Practically brawny. She had the type of body that could have real, natural strength if she put forth even a modicum of effort. But she never had, so it didn't. The burden on her back—the sheer resistance to her effort—was staggering. She balked. "Oh my God. People do this for fun?"

"That's what I said!"

Panic flooded through Josie. It hadn't occurred to her that they might not be physically capable of this trip. "How are we supposed to carry these for three days?"

Neena shook her head. "I have no idea."

"How?"

"I don't know," Neena said. But the joking had stopped. Whenever one of them freaked out—and, admittedly, it was usually Josie—the other went calm. "We just will."

Josie was sure that if Neena could have shrugged right now, she would have shrugged. Not condescendingly. The gesture would have been comforting. Josie's panic dulled back into an uneasy, unidentifiable dread. "Right. People do this all the time."

"Yeah. And we're people," Neena said. "Surely we can do this, too."

"Did you see us in gym class?"

Neena slammed the hatch closed. Birds squawked and took to the humid air. "I kept my eyes closed in gym class."

"That explains a lot."

After double-checking that they had everything, Josie stuffed the car keys into the top of Neena's pack.

"Oh, jeez," Neena said. "Don't look."

Moving to investigate, Josie whacked Neena with her pack. "What?"

Neena oofed.

"Sorry. What? I don't see any— Oh."

"I told you not to look."

A plywood notice board stood beside the trail. In large type on a sheet of copy paper protected by plastic, a faded sign read: BEAR CANISTERS REQUIRED.

"It's okay," Neena said. "We've got one."

A second notice with smaller type was tacked beside it, and Josie toddled over to read it. The unwelcome words raked across her skin so viciously that she felt marked. "It says if we don't have a canister we can get fined. Or even get jail time."

"Again. We have a canister."

"It's from the Forest Service. 'Emergency requirement to use bear-resistant canisters in . . .'. And great. It lists Frazier Mountain, Deep Fork, Misty Rock Wilderness, and Burnt Balsam Knob. That's our whole itinerary."

Neena sidled up to her and pointed. "What are those?" Several different sets of handwriting were scrawled directly onto the splintered plywood.

5/20 *bear walked through Misty Rock campsite at 9:40* PM

6/2 *Meadow Ridge Cove 2x bears*

6-9 *saw one bear cross Misty Rock Creek*

6/17 *meadow ridge cove 1 bear 6 pm*

6/29 *one bear in Misty Rock Wilderness*

7-7 *Burnt Balsam 2 bears*

Josie's head wrenched away, trying to avoid absorbing the information. Primal anxiety swelled within. In her mind, a lumbering beast snuffled outside their flimsy tent. The hackles of its shadow rose. A ferocious claw slashed through the defenseless nylon, attacking with frenzied black eyes and snarling white teeth.

"No activity since July," Neena said. "See? They're already hibernating."

"We're so getting *Revenant*-ed."

"That was a movie."

"Based on a true story!"

"Okay, but it happened, like, two hundred years ago in Canada or Alaska or whatever. And he was attacked by a grizzly bear. No one gets hurt by black bears."

Actually, in this decade alone, ten people had been killed by black bears in North America. Josie had looked it up. None of them had been on this part of the continent, but still. In recent years, black bear traffic had increased significantly throughout Asheville. Heavy rains due to climate change meant it took longer for nuts and berries to ripen, which meant that bears were emerging from the woods in search of other food. Trash cans were gashed with claw marks. People were hospitalized after accidentally interrupting feasts. And then there was the man who had weaponized his own mountain bike to fend off an aggressive mama bear. That had happened here, inside this very forest. Where there were no cars or houses or buildings to provide protective shelter.

"Oh, shit." Neena punched Josie's arm. "Smokey Bear. How did we forget him? He's a park ranger. He saves lives. Think of them as helpful Smokeys."

But Josie didn't want to think about bears at all. She desperately wanted to *stop* thinking about them. She couldn't admit, not even to Neena, that *The Wizard of Oz* had frightened her as a child—not because of the Wicked Witch or her squadron of flying monkeys, but when Dorothy and her friends had chanted, "Lions and tigers and bears! Oh my!" as they'd skipped into the dark wood, they had introduced Josie to the concept of being eaten alive. Flesh ripping. Teeth gnashing. Watching your own meaty chunks be swallowed down the throat of another carnivorous mammal.

Lions . . .

Black panthers had long been part of state folklore, but they were as likely to be discovered as Bigfoot. Bobcats did live here, though they only attacked humans if they were sick or rabid. However, once upon a time, mountain lions had also lived here—and some believed they still did. Sightings of long-tailed cats with tawny-colored fur remained rampant among hunters, though experts claimed if they did exist, they were simply exotic pets that had been released. This didn't make Josie feel any better. A pet mountain lion was still a mountain lion.

. . . and tigers . . .

At least there weren't any tigers. Although Josie had once read that there were more tigers in captivity in the United States than in the wilds of Asia, a fact that distressed her on multiple counts.

. . . and bears!

But bears. There were definitely bears out here. *Oh my.*

Josie shifted to her mental checklist: *Keep the campsite clean. Make noise. Place everything that smells out of reach. Watch out for scat and tracks and rubbed tree bark. Urinate far away from the tent.* Her palms were clammy. She didn't want to do this. Why were they doing this?

"Where's your phone?" Neena asked. "We need to commemorate the moment." She nodded toward the other sign, the one beside the notice board. It was large and proud and distinctly American with its National Forest typeface and specific shade of brown.

WADE HARTE TRAILHEAD, it said. PISGAH NATIONAL FOREST.

Josie tugged the phone out from her jeans—her hip belt didn't have a handy pocket like Neena's—and they took dozens of selfies in front of the sign, hoping that at least one would make them look good. Giant smiles. Sunglasses on, sunglasses off. The screen blurred because Josie's glasses were prescription. To conserve the battery, she switched the phone to airplane mode, and then Neena stowed it in the top of Josie's pack so that it wouldn't dig into her thigh. It barely fit. Josie wondered if the weight would lighten as they consumed the food or if it would grow heavier with their exhaustion.

"Nothing to it but to do it," Neena said, quoting their least-favorite teacher because they liked reminding each other how awful he was.

"Keep calm and carry on," Josie said as they set off down the trail.

"Too blessed to be stressed."

"Oh God. Why do they all have to rhyme?"

Their banter continued as they rounded the first bend. Josie glanced back. The burbling river softened and then silenced. Neena's car disappeared.

The woods swallowed them whole.

ROBUST EVERGREENS TOWERED overhead and deciduous hardwoods preened, dappling the midday light. Rhododendrons spiraled with leathery leaves. Wildflowers dipped their heads in greeting. *Those*, smooth and red. *These*, frilly and white. A weedy vine tangled to form a wall of electric-orange blooms. It was a dramatic contrast from the tired vegetation that had edged the parking lot, yellowed by car exhaust and human presence. The inner forest was lush and vigorously alive. Even the air smelled better here, pristine with fresh oxygen and perfumed by rainy loam.

Neena would have been awed . . . if only her backpack wasn't trying to murder her.

The Wade Harte Trail had been challenging from the start. It began with a climb and then continued to a steeper climb. The ascent was unrelenting. Roots, rocks, and downed trees were scattered everywhere across the path, treacherous obstacles lying in wait to roll their ankles. It was exactly what Neena had expected but also somehow worse. Hunching and huffing beneath her pack, its straps dug nastily into her shoulders. No amount of adjusting them or cinching the belt helped. Her limbs dragged with unparalleled fatigue. They had been walking for eight minutes.

"Fuuuuuuuuuck," Neena said, for the fifth time.

"At least we're only doing half the trail. Can you imagine?"

"Who is Wade Harte, anyway?"

"No idea, but I read somewhere"—though neither girl had much life experience, they'd always read something, somewhere—"that hikers call this a mini-AT."

"A mini-what?"

"Appalachian Trail." Josie pronounced it correctly, like a Southerner. *Latch-un*, not *lay-shun*.

"Oh. Doesn't that run nearby? Or am I thinking of the Mountains-to-Sea Trail?"

"Both, I think."

Neena bragged. "Look at us, knowing stuff about hiking."

"We're hiking geniuses."

The girls were traipsing up Frazier Mountain, the tallest of several mountains that crested six thousand feet in these woods, but they weren't hiking to its peak. Thank God. They planned to ascend two-thirds of the way up the mountain before descending into a clearing called Deep Fork, where they would set up camp and spend the night. Measured from the parking lot, the elevation gain was over two thousand feet.

Due to the ascent, today's hike would be more physically challenging, but tomorrow's mileage would be more than double. In the morning, they would head into the Misty Rock Wilderness, which sounded like a location on a Tolkien map, and then eat lunch at Burnt Balsam Knob, which sounded like a penis that had been caught in a forest fire. After that, they'd turn around and come back, looping onto a different trail for scenic variation. Tomorrow night, they'd sleep somewhere back in the Misty Rock Wilderness before returning to the trailhead on Wednesday afternoon.

Round trip, the journey was nearly twenty miles. A through-hike on the Wade Harte was just over thirty—stretching from Frazier Mountain in the north to the town of Brevard in the south—but Neena and Josie had wanted this trip to be theirs, completely. They didn't want another person dropping them off at one end and picking them up at the other.

The trail would eventually cross through a protected wilderness area where signs and trail markers weren't allowed, but, so far, the path had been well-worn and easy to follow. Neena prided herself on a strong internal compass. Her parents, however, had also made them pack an actual compass, a printed trail map, and further print-outs about the trail sections and water sources.

But mainly they were relying on technology. Their phones already had compass apps, and GPS was even easier.

Neena wobbled over another supine tree decomposing across the trail. Behind her, Josie's footsteps halted. "Did you look?" Josie asked.

"At what?"

"You should always look before stepping over a log. In case of snakes."

Neena shuffled around to face her, wielding a deadly stare.

"I know." Josie blushed as she peered over the log. "But seriously, timber rattlesnakes and copperheads. You need to be careful."

Neena wondered if their entire trip would be peppered with these lists of lethal fauna. She changed the subject to something far more pressing. "I need to pee."

Josie's response was exuberant. "Yes! I'm dying, but I was afraid to say something. I mean, if it weren't for the trees, we'd still be able to see your car."

The girls had "pre-hydrated"—they despised this word, cudgeled into the English language by coaches and jocks—by consuming a liter of water each on the road. Supposedly, this would give them a head start on fluid loss. Win had advised them to drink slowly, because chugging would make the liquid pass faster, but that didn't seem to have mattered. Their bladders were already bursting.

Neena unsnapped the sternum strap and hip belt, slid out, and gasped as the pack almost ripped her arms from their sockets. The pack thudded straight to the ground. She teetered with the drastic shift in her center of gravity.

Josie made a similar gasp and teeter.

"Okay," Neena said, massaging her shoulders. "We'll find a better way to do that." But the freedom was rapturous. They were like a sagging mule team lugging supplies into the Grand Canyon. Two liters of water per day, per person, was required, so they'd secured one-liter bottles to both sides of each pack, which they planned to refill along the way. Only luck had kept the bottles from cracking in the fall.

"Do you need the shovel?" Josie asked.

"Thankfully"—Neena shuddered—"not yet." Win had been remarkably unperturbed as he'd given them the instructions about defecating in the woods.

"Toilet paper or are you gonna air-dry?"

"We have to bury it if we use it, right?"

Josie scratched behind an ear. "Probably?"

They decided to air-dry.

Neena climbed uphill, off the path, and ducked behind a boulder—but not before first checking for venomous snakes. *Damn you, Josie.* Positioning herself so that the stream would travel downhill, Neena tugged her jeans and underwear down to her knees.

The forest canopy swayed overhead. The wind chilled her exposed flesh.

Josie piped up from behind a nearby conifer. "I read that this land used to be part of the Biltmore Estate, and the Vanderbilts were the ones who sold it to the Forest Service." The Biltmore was the largest privately owned house in the United States, and, at the time of its construction, the Vanderbilts were the country's wealthiest family thanks to the fortune they'd made in shipping and railroads. Now their house was Asheville's main tourist attraction. It looked like the *Downton Abbey* house on steroids. "Apparently, Pisgah was one of the first national forests in the east."

"How was this even theirs to sell? Surely, it belonged to the Cherokees." Neena's parents were Indian, but strangers often mistook this for American Indian, which, around here, meant Cherokee. Unless they presumed her family was Mexican. Which also happened to a ludicrous degree.

"Surely."

"What does 'Pisgah' even mean? It sounds so ugly. I used to think it was *Pig*-sah."

"I did, too," Josie said. "I think it's biblical."

Neena's squat was careful. Her legs trembled. Nature finally overtook performance anxiety, and she sighed with relief as the trickle turned into a gush. But when she waved her hips to shake off, a watery red droplet splashed onto her thigh. "Shit," she whispered.

"What?" Josie called out.

"When you're done, I need the toilet paper."

"Oh, you *have to shit*. I thought you saw something."

"No," Neena said. "I'm spotting."

"Oh! Shit."

Neena's period wasn't supposed to start for another week. Hopefully, this was as heavy as her flow would get. Foliage rustled, footsteps scuffled, and a pack unzipped. Josie hustled up the bank. "I have something better," she said. An arm materialized around the boulder holding out a puffy object in a rosy pink wrapper.

The sight instantly soothed Neena. "You're a gem."

"Be prepared," Josie said. "The Boy Scouts were talking about menstruation, right? I'm not looking," she added, shuffling backward until Neena could grab it.

Neena was grateful they subscribed to the same philosophy regarding privacy. While they didn't mind peeing beside each other in public stalls, neither wanted to be seen with her pants down. Their philosophies split, however, when it came to products. Though a real pad was far superior to folded toilet paper, Neena still felt as if she were wearing an adult diaper. But Josie's periods were lighter, and Neena knew tampons were uncomfortable for her—Josie said it was like hard-packing her vagina with dry cotton balls.

It was a lot to know about another girl, but Neena Chandrasekhar and Josie Gordon were as familiar with each other's cycles as they were with their own, having been best friends since freshman year.

They'd attended the same middle school but had only known each other by name. That changed one day when their Honors Biology teacher had removed his scuffed dress shoes to display an eleventh toe. While the other students scrambled from their lab chairs in a mad rush to gawk, Neena and Josie's disbelieving eyes had met across the room as if to say, *What does this have to do with dissecting fetal pigs?*

The funny and bizarre often kick-started great friendships.

Before they found each other, they'd had different best friends, but those attachments had fallen apart around the same time. As their exes rose into bigger crowds—Neena's to the cross-county team, Josie's to a group of girls who didn't *do* anything, but who were moderately more attractive—Neena and Josie became a new twosome. To this day, they still talked about Grace and Sarah the way others might pore over a painful romantic breakup. Because that's what it had felt like to lose the person who had once been each girl's *most important* person. The losses were devastating.

Though their bond had strengthened over being dumped, it was solidified by a shared sense of humor and passion for the same TV shows. Josie was the first classmate Neena had met who not only watched all the best current sitcoms, but all the old ones, too. They were willing to try anything from any country or decade. They loved good comedy with the fervor of televangelists. Josie didn't even mind whenever Neena insisted on listening to the commentary features, and it was within these tracks that Neena had begun to realize *people* were making these shows—*writers*, not just the actors and comedians in front of the camera. Neena wanted to be one of those people.

Her plan was to major in economics at USC, but to study film and television production on the side. Maybe, eventually, she could even convince her parents to let her double major. Because what she wanted more than anything was to be a showrunner someday—to write and sell a pilot and have her hand in every aspect of its production. And she was willing to work twice as hard as the other students, pursuing two careers at once, if it kept her parents happy.

They didn't hide that they would have rather she attend MIT, like her brother, Darshan, or at least—*at least*—one of the Ivy Leagues. It embarrassed Neena that her parents fell into this cliché. Briefly, she had even considered disguising her intentions, but she wasn't the type of teenager who lied to her parents. And, perhaps because of this honesty, they had reluctantly given their support.

Her father had instilled a love of comedy in Neena, but this time it was her mother who had argued on Neena's behalf. *What did you expect, filling her head with Mindy Kaling and that* Fleabag *woman, day after day?* Ma had said to him, her stacked bangles jangling with each emotional finger jab. And Neena had been granted permission to study film production as long as it didn't interfere with her economics classes.

Despite this, she was afraid. Soon she would be dropped off in America's second-most-populous city, and she would be alone. No Ma and Baba. No Josie. She was scared to move somewhere so unfamiliar, and she was scared of not being able to make any new friends. People in LA were undeniably more sophisticated and worldly, and she worried that she would appear plain and backwoods by comparison. That the other students would all have better clothes than her, better skin, better hair.

But, most of all, Neena was afraid of failure. Of not being good enough and getting stuck in the economics department forever. Or maybe being *just* good enough to find employment someday as a writer's assistant, but never good enough to climb any higher.

She also feared that if she admitted any of this to her parents, they would change their minds about letting her go. And whenever she broached the topic with Josie, Josie quickly shut it down with tight-lipped petulance. Because even though everything felt scary, she knew it was also exciting. One day, it would even feel normal.

Meanwhile, Josie would still be living in this version of normal. The depressed mother, the filthy house. It was why Neena kept trying—to buoy Josie's mood, to keep her active and *doing*. Not only had this trip been Neena's idea, but she'd also had to reach for her pack first. Step onto the trail first. Hell, she'd even had to announce her intention to pee first.

As Neena zipped up her pants, Josie's gaze remained tactfully averted. They trudged back down the bank, and then Neena tucked the empty pink wrapper into her top pouch. All trash had to be carried out of the forest.

Neither girl wanted to struggle into her pack again.

"Do we really need food? Or water? Or shelter?" Neena asked.

Josie squinched her nose in concentration. "There's a correct way to do this. I know it. We just have to remember."

Neena stood aside, idle and useless, while Josie grunted through several flawed attempts. But then, miraculously, she hoisted her pack onto a knee, turned her upper body sideways, slipped the pack onto one shoulder and then efficiently onto the other.

"How'd you do that?" Neena asked, despite witnessing the marvel.

Josie beamed. The thirty-something pounds of discomfort only mildly tarnished her smile. "Told you it had something to do with the knees."

She guided Neena into the lavender pack, and they basked in newfound confidence. Their endorphins were finally kicking in. The righteous pleasure of their hard work was certain to propel them up the rest of the mountainside.

It wasn't to be. Once again, the trail was instantly grueling. Nonstop switchbacks kept the incline constant and demanding. Twenty feet up from their resting place, Neena gasped—bug-eyed and wretchedly out of shape. Her clothes, muddied from earlier in the parking lot, were drenched with sweat. No doubt this trip would be a disaster, but, even so, Neena was still hoping for a *lighthearted* disaster. At the very least, this would make a funny story she could tell at parties. Assuming she ever started going to parties. Her borrowed boots slipped on a tottering rock. Her heart catapulted in panic.

"Are you okay?" Josie asked behind her.

Neena steadied herself and held up a hand that meant, *Yes, too breathless to speak.*

As her best friend literally walked her first mile in somebody else's shoes, Josie tromped forward in her own. Her sturdy hiking shoes, more like sneakers than boots, had only been worn twice, including today. They had been preserved in closet dust ever since her mother, in one of her sporadic attempts to *be* a mother, decided they needed to get out of the house. She had surprised Josie with a name-brand pair, purchased off the clearance rack at DSW. They had driven out of the city to hike, but, after only a few steps toward Looking Glass Rock, her mother had crumpled into the dirt. Inconsolable. Win had to pick them up because Josie was afraid to drive. Later, she learned the trail had been one of her father's regular haunts. Now these mountains felt haunted in a different way.

The untested shoes pinched her toes and rubbed her heels. Josie comforted herself by remembering the Band-Aids. If necessary, they could be slapped over any blisters later tonight. She had packed more than enough for three days.

The girls were returning home on Wednesday because Thursday was Josie's freshman orientation. Unlike Neena, Josie had no idea what she wanted to study. She wasn't excited about college. It felt like being sentenced to four more years of high school. Though her situation wasn't uncommon—most teenagers didn't know what they wanted to do with their lives—it was impossible not to compare herself to her best friend, and it was inevitable that she had interpreted this uncertainty as a personal shortcoming.

But, secretly, Josie wondered if this trip was about to change everything. This wasn't as outlandish as it sounded. It wasn't unreasonable to hope that her passion might turn out to be the same one as the rest of her family. Surely the outdoors coursed through her blood, too; she'd only been denied the opportunity to discover it. Josie imagined these mountains becoming her sanctuary. Envisioned herself as such a natural that she would be mystically compelled to through-hike the Appalachian Trail, like in *A Walk in the Woods*, or the Pacific Crest Trail, like in *Wild*. Would this trip be the turning point when she stopped envying everyone else's adventures and started having her own?

The trail dipped unexpectedly. Josie fell.

Neena spun around at the sharp cry. "Oh my God. Are you okay?"

The pack was so huge that the spill didn't hurt. Josie landed on padding. But the drop had startled her, and unwanted tears sprung to her eyes. "I'm fine. I'm fine." She laughed to disguise her embarrassment. *Of course I'm the one who can't catch herself*, she thought, conveniently forgetting Neena's incident in the parking lot. Her mind was skilled at self-sabotage. "Uh, remind me again why we're here?"

"Because we're becoming one with nature. We're soaking in Gaia's bounty! And tonight, we'll sleep beneath the stars like . . . sumptuous pagan goddesses."

"This backpack," Josie said as Neena helped her stand, "does make me feel mega Zen."

Neena burst into laughter. Her outrageous cackle had been the soundtrack to their entire friendship. Normally, it was Josie's favorite music. But in her humiliation, it grated.

The path worn into the mountain was only one person wide, and, as always, Josie fell in line behind Neena. An ancient oak surveilled them from the woodsy depths. The unusual tree was stripped bare—struck by lightning or disease, Josie couldn't tell. A single arthritic branch remained, pointing like a crooked arm and knobby forefinger back the way they came. A strange revulsion drifted over her.

"Maybe it's just because hiking is terrible," she said, "but doesn't it look like that tree is telling us to go back?"

"That tree is an asshole," Neena said.

The forest returned to tranquility. Strenuous, laborious tranquility. Panting and puffing and chattering like wheezy songbirds, the girls crossed through a velveteen outcrop of mossy green boulders. Ferns carpeted the shady groves. Tumbling cascades of a nearby stream, present but unseen, were amplified throughout the canopy.

The combination of sublime beauty and severe exhaustion began to soften Josie's fatalism. A tenuous but arresting sense of empowerment manifested in its place, and, although she didn't realize it, the same sensation was happening inside Neena. It was their first taste of adulthood. A preview of what was to be forever. They were here without parents, teachers, or supervisors. They were going to feed themselves and build their own shelter, and no one could tell them where to go or what to do.

Gnawing disquiet gradually slowed Josie's pace. Her instincts perceived the subtle shifts in the trees before her ears understood: shuffling leaves and crunching dead wood.

She stopped. Stiffened.

The faint noises grew more distinct. Neena halted. She glanced back at Josie, and the girls exchanged mirrored expressions of wide-eyed alarm.

Josie's nerves pulsated. *Bear.*

A man's timbre rumbled down the mountainside. But as Josie slackened with relief, Neena compressed with fear. The voice was heading toward them, broadening and becoming cavernous. The southern half of the trail was often used for day hikes because it was easily accessible from the parkway, but the northern half, their half, was less traveled. More isolated. It wasn't that Neena hadn't expected to run into anybody out here, but the sudden approach of an unknown man cowed her. She felt disarmed in the most literal sense—like his presence stripped away any weapons she thought she'd had.

The voice grew louder.

Neena couldn't pick out any of his words, only his tone. The boom was commanding and confident. Almost sardonic. It reduced her back into a child.

"I'm sure it's fine," Josie said, although doubt had already crept in. "He's probably someone like Win."

Immobilized by dread, Neena didn't respond. Humans were far more dangerous than bears. She knew plenty of stories about hikers who had disappeared, plucked off the earth by their own careless mishaps . . . or by other hikers.

"I used to think that if I said hello to somebody," the voice said, "and they didn't respond . . ."

Josie gestured toward the trees. Neena nodded but then shook her head. It's what they *should* have done—hidden—but the voice was too close now. They were out of time. Neena strained to listen for the sounds of a woman, hoping he wasn't talking to another man. Or worse, himself. But *was* that worse? Would she rather run into two men or one possibly deranged man?

". . . it meant I was a ghost," the voice finished.

He emerged into view. Neena shuddered from the release of tension. His companion was a girl, and he wasn't even a man. They were teenagers, maybe twenty at the oldest. The atmosphere brightened. The trees shook out their nervous leaves.

"I'd love to see a ghost," the girl said.

"But that's the problem," the boy said. "Nobody *could* see me."

The two jumped as they rounded the switchback, startled to discover Neena and Josie on the other side. "Oh! We didn't see you," the girl said, which made her laugh. An accidental callback. They both looked at ease, the type of people who hiked difficult trails and made their own gorp. Neither wore a backpacking pack, but the boy had an enviably small daypack. He was white, and the girl's features were East Asian. Her hair was pinned up in a thick crown braid. A Heidi milkmaid braid.

"I like your hair," Josie said. Her own strawberry blonde locks were in two long plaits—a much more simple style. Josie usually wore her hair loose or in a ponytail, and Neena suspected she'd done the braids to look outdoorsy. It was cute, though. Sweet. Neena's black hair was snipped into a blunt bob, too short to do anything but hang.

Heidi's smile grew. "Thanks."

Normally, this was when the two parties would nod and move along, but a conversation had already been started. It seemed polite to talk a little bit longer.

"Are you headed to the summit?" the boy asked. He was tall and strapping, and his irises sparkled in a warm chestnut brown. The whole package reminded Neena of Win. A long time ago, she'd had a crush on Win. If she was being honest, she still did, though not in any serious way. Just in the way that when he was around, he was pleasing to look at. Perhaps for this reason, Neena felt tongue-tied.

"No," Josie said. "We're doing the Wade Harte."

Neena was glad when Josie didn't clarify they were only doing part of the Wade Harte, and equally glad that the couple didn't comment about how defeated they already looked. These two must have arrived at the crack of dawn to have already summited and be on their way back down. Neena felt envious that their torture was almost over.

Concern flickered across the boy's face. "You aren't staying in Deep Fork tonight, are you?"

"Yeah." Josie frowned. "Why?"

"Oh man. You haven't heard?" When the girls gave him a puzzled look, he glanced at Heidi. Her eyes flashed a warning at him.

"Heard what?" Josie asked.

"No, nothing. It's fine. It's just . . ." The boy appeared torn between regret at bringing it up and a pressing need to continue.

Unconsciously, Neena leaned in. "Weird stuff happens there," he finished. "Be careful, is all I'm saying."

"What kind of weird stuff?" she asked. Voice rediscovered.

"Unexplained noises in the night. Items stolen from tents."

Neena's pulse thumped.

"A buddy of mine once swore that someone took a picture of him while he was sleeping." As the boy gripped the straps of his backpack, his eyes darted into the woods behind them. "He'd been out here hiking solo, and he didn't find it on his phone until he got home. I would have thought he was messing with me, except his hands were shaking when he showed me the picture. He looked dead asleep in it . . . I don't know." His cadence was changing, dropping into a redneck lilt. "Some folks say when the mist creeps in after midnight, there's a man who likes to play tricks on campers—"

Heidi thwacked him across the chest. "He's joking," she said as he collapsed into laughter. "I'm sorry. My boyfriend has a horrible sense of humor." And then to him, "God, you almost had me, too. You're such a dick." But she grinned as she scolded him.

"Sorry," he said to Neena. "I couldn't resist."

The hot shame of gullibility flared inside her. But then she was laughing, too. She admired his boldness and showmanship. Josie glanced at her, less amused, as their bodies all shifted and resumed walking—interaction complete.

"Safe travels," Heidi called from behind them.

"Lock your tent flaps," the boy said.

As soon as they were out of earshot, Josie muttered, "That was odd."

"I liked him. I thought it was funny."

"Really?" Josie's brow wrinkled. "He reminded me of my brother."

Neena was grateful that her dark brown skin could hide a blush. "Speaking of photos," she said, backpedaling, and they took another series of selfies to mark their progress. This time, their screened reflections were disheveled. Distant. And when Neena tucked her phone away again, her hand felt naked. Even in a relaxed state, her fingers were still gripped as if they were holding a rectangle. Nurture overtaking nature. The compulsion arose to Google if other people had this problem, too, but she knew she couldn't.

For a moment, Neena wished they could turn around and follow the couple out. She wanted to slump in her car and lose herself in the comfort of her phone. But Josie was behind her, as always, and the thought of abandoning this trip that she herself had insisted on made her feel guilty. And then resentful for feeling guilty.

The girls slogged deeper into the lonesome infinity of forest.

THEY KEPT PLODDING, kept resting. The humid air became moist rather than fresh, and the water they drank evaporated into sweat that attracted hovering clouds of gnats. Stagnant pockets of the unseen stream bred and released mosquitos. Their arms itched with round, angry bites. Despite their being on a mountainside, there were no views. No sweeping vistas. The trees and rhododendrons enclosed them in a cramped realm.

Uneasiness settled underneath Josie's skin. It was as if something was watching them from behind the trees, always ducking out of sight before she could name it. When the stream finally did reveal itself, the girls crossed it, and then they crossed it again a half hour later. Sometime after, a small—almost trivial—grassy clearing appeared, which Josie guessed was an empty campsite . . . which made her realize she wasn't even positive what a campsite was *supposed* to look like.

Neena didn't seem concerned. "I'm sure it'll be obvious later."

They trekked beside a third prong of the stream, one that was wider and prettier, and declared themselves overdue for their first real break with sitting. Glorious, glorious sitting. Proud of their cleverness, the girls shed their packs by backing up and releasing them onto waist-high boulders.

Neena inhaled with pleasure. The water warbled in an agreeable manner. "Is a creek the same thing as a stream? Or do you think there's a scientific difference?"

"I don't know." Josie removed her phone from its zippered prison. A comforting rush swept over her hand, which had been tingling with emptiness since the trailhead. "I'll look it up— Oh."

Neena laughed once through her nose. "I keep doing that, too."

"How did anyone know anything before the internet?"

"Our parents were idiots."

"Or," Josie said, "were they smarter because they actually had to retain information?"

"No."

"Your parents, maybe."

"No," Neena repeated. "We're smarter because we figured out a way where we don't *have* to."

"We are so smart to have figured that out."

"We should figure out," Neena said, "where we packed the snacks."

The snacks were near the top of Josie's pack, where she had carefully separated out this afternoon's allocation—two single-serving bags of chips and a sandwich-size Ziploc of dried apricots—from the rest of their food. The chips were Cheetos and Nacho Cheese Doritos because the girls believed in chips that stained their fingertips orange. It was only a coincidence that the fruit was orange, too.

Josie had been in charge of snacks because she had the snack house. Neena had the meal house. When Josie's father was alive, her parents had bought from bulk bins and had cooked giant pots of organic comfort food. Naturally, Josie had developed a taste for junk. Now she missed the rice and beans. Her mother shopped only sporadically, and the groceries were haphazard, as if she'd forgotten the purpose of shopping. Though she still patronized the same stores as before, everything became convenient to consume. Josie's kitchen cabinets were scattered with nuts and bananas and granola—squirrel food—while an under-the-bed tub in her bedroom was stuffed with Frito-Lay variety packs and Campbell's soup and Top Ramen, purchased with her Kmart employee discount.

The girls washed their hands with globs of sanitizer and settled onto a flat boulder that touched the stream. Unlike the other rocks, which wore fuzzy sweaters of verdant moss, this rock was bare and had perfect indentations for two human bottoms. Trees dipped their exposed roots into the water as it flowed and bubbled past. The girls' matching blue stones of lapis lazuli shimmered in the refracted light, but Josie's swollen finger throbbed around her ring. Her aching feet groaned in her shoes.

"This part, I understand," Neena said. "This part where I'm sitting."

"The whole thing should be this part."

"Remember when we thought camping—staying in *one place* for *three whole days*—would be boring?"

Josie loosened her laces. "We were so naive. Staying in one place is the best."

They divvied up the bounty by mixing the chips half-and-half. The apricots were placed between them. To Josie, dried fruit tasted like sadness and neglect, but today it was as delicious as candy because it gave her another reason not to move.

Her first bottle of water was already a third empty, so she took prudent sips, luxuriating as it swelled and replenished her cells. She and Neena would refill their bottles at a spring near the campsite tonight. Neither wanted to refill now because they didn't want to carry the extra weight. Neena downed the rest of her first bottle. Recklessly, she unscrewed the lid off her second and began to chug.

"Hey!" Josie stopped her. "Save some for later."

"I am."

"I know, but . . . save some *extra*. For *in case*."

"In case of what?"

"Anything," Josie said.

"You are such a mom," Neena said, thinking of her own mother and realizing belatedly that she'd made the slam worse. She cringed but didn't apologize. She was embarrassed, but she also worried that acknowledging the subject might hurt Josie further. Unlike Josie's mom, Neena's was constantly butting in with her concerns, thoughts, and opinions. It was maddening, but Neena knew enough to be grateful.

Ma was the only person besides Josie who texted her regularly. Though she worked considerable hours as a neurologist, she was always available by phone. This afternoon was already the longest they'd gone without talking in . . . who knew how many years. Forever. This trip was a trial run for their upcoming separation. Except, even then, they would still be texting and FaceTiming.

Neena glossed over her blunder by stretching out on the rock. "Oh my God." Her tormented muscles whimpered in relief. "Lying down is even better. You have to try this."

"I'll never get up if I lie down," Josie said as she lowered herself.

They ate on their backs like otters, orange crumbs littering their bellies and chests, pacified by the babbling stream and its soft, cooling aroma. Neena sniffed the breeze. The scent was rich with minerals. Compared to Josie, Neena was always more aware of her breath.

Her asthma required two puffs in the morning and two at night on a steroid inhaler, and she had a rescue inhaler for when she was sick or before exercise. She'd used the rescue inhaler on the drive here, so her lungs were okay. Of greater concern were the bruises she felt blossoming below her shoulder blades.

Her head turned toward Josie. "Oh no. Are you a little pink?"

Josie bolted upright, pressing her thumb into her forearm. A white print was left behind. Swearing, she scuttled off the rock and fumbled through her pack. Her skin was fair and freckled and already slathered in SPF.

"Maybe it's just warm from the exercise," Neena said.

"No," Josie said, reapplying. "I'm definitely burning."

The chemical tang of sunscreen mixed into the air. Neena examined the bottle without picking it up because she didn't want to get her hands greasy. "A *hundred*?"

Josie snorted. "SPF 100+. Don't forget the 'plus'—it's important."

Neena shook her head when Josie offered the bottle. She was also already wearing some, and the whole trail had been in the shade. She was fine. Josie packed up the sunscreen along with their empty food bags. The sight made Neena flinch. "My hips hurt," she said. "And my back." *We don't have to leave now, do we?*

"Mine too," Josie said. "And my feet." *Hell no.*

They watched the water. After a few minutes, Josie began to wander and collect stones. Neena observed as Josie stacked the pile, biggest to littlest, into a satisfying decorative cairn. She croaked to her feet and joined in. Selecting, balancing. The process was both meditative and addictive, like solving a puzzle. Soon the girls had constructed an entire village out of stacked stone—a hamlet overlooking the sea. They took dozens of photographs from every angle. Neena admired their sprawling creation with pride.

"Godzilla time." Josie reached out to topple the stacks.

Neena thrust out both hands to stop her. "What are you doing?"

"Leave No Trace." When Neena didn't respond, Josie went on. "Leave No Trace? It's a thing. Like, an ethical code of honor. You've really never heard of it?"

Neena had not.

"It means that whatever you bring into nature, you carry out. It doesn't only apply to garbage. You're supposed to leave everything the way you found it. So, if we let these stones stand, we'd be leaving behind proof of human impact. It'd be like carving our names into a tree. Or throwing the Doritos bag into the ferns."

"But . . ." Neena hesitated. Wondering if this made her a lesser person. "What if I *like* the idea of leaving something behind?"

"Then you'd be ruining the view for the next people who sat here."

Josie's pronouncement felt harsh—that their pretty stone towers could ruin anybody's view.

"Imagine if everybody who sat here left one of these," she continued. "This place would be nothing *but* stacked stones. It'd be the same as a crowd of people."

"Okay," Neena said, "so the next hiker who sits here gets peeved and knocks them down. Who cares? Just . . . let's not do it ourselves."

"We're not leaving them."

"Why not?"

"Because I just said!"

There was a burst of irritated silence. Once again, it was like being trapped in a loop with her mother. Neena hated feeling like a child.

"Fine," Neena said. Childishly. "Whatever."

Resisting the urge to add that moving rocks around could also contribute to erosion, Josie tried to spin the ring on her index finger, a nervous habit. The ring didn't budge. Her fingers had fattened into sausages, swollen from hanging at her sides during the hike.

"How about we leave one?" she finally said. "This one." She

pointed to Neena's tallest cairn. "I like the round stone on top. It seems like it should roll away, but it doesn't."

Neena shrugged.

Josie sighed. But correctly interpreting the ennui as acceptance, she dismantled the nearest tower. The rocks tumbled to the earth and splooshed into the water.

Neena joined in the demolition until they were all gone except the one. "You sure?" she asked, rearing back to kick it.

"Don't," Josie said.

"I wasn't going to," Neena lied. She glanced at her phone, which was still in her hand. "*Shit*. It's a quarter till five."

Josie was equally startled. "What?"

The girls had read that the average backpacker could hike two miles per hour, including breaks, so they'd lowered their own estimation to one and a half. This meant that with three hours of hiking— plenty of padding for their 4.2-mile day—they would arrive at their destination around 5:45 p.m., which would give them three additional hours to set up camp, make dinner, and hang out before it got dark. Sunset was at 8:15, but Win said they'd have light on the mountain for at least an additional half hour.

Neena flushed with stress. "I knew we were behind schedule, but . . . How many miles have we hiked so far?"

"Almost two," Josie said.

Neena erupted. "Not even half?" She did the math, calculating from the time they'd left the trailhead. "We're traveling less than a mile per hour." Panic made her turn on Josie again. "You've had your phone out since we stopped here. Why didn't you notice how slowly we were traveling?"

"So have you! Why didn't *you* notice?"

Neena didn't like the accusation directed back onto her. It was neither of their faults. Or they were both at fault. Whatever. "Okay," she said, trying to convince herself as much as Josie. "We're okay. We'll be fine." True, they would no longer have any time to relax at the campsite, but they could still easily make it there before dark. Neena squirmed at the thought of *not* making it before dark.

"Yeah." Josie sounded even less assured as they strapped into their packs. "We'll just walk a little faster."

Their spirits picked up in earnest as, at long last, the elevation took a dip. Unfortunately, this downhill respite was only a blink before the trail resumed its murderous ascent. The girls tunneled upward through a dense tract of mountain laurel. Branches on either side of the path interlocked overhead, creating a human-size passageway that canopied them in flora. Green sunlight strained through the leaves.

Time marched forward as their pace slowed down. The tunnel was endless and claustrophobic. Out of breath, they had no choice but to take frequent breaks. After an hour—around the time they had originally planned to reach their campsite—the climb intensified. The incline grew hellishly steep. The terrain became rockier.

It felt more precarious, which forced their steps to be more cautious.

Another hour passed. Despite the perspiration and heat and suffering, Neena felt the temperature begin to drop. A warning of the night to come. They'd planned for three hours at camp before nightfall, but now they were looking at half that.

Their salvation would arrive in the form of a spring, which would also be their water source for the night. Shortly after the spring, the path would fork—the trail to Frazier Mountain's summit on one side, the Wade Harte Trail on the other. Their instructions were to take a right, and then the Deep Fork campsite would be immediately ahead. But as Neena peeked through a rare break in the tangled thicket, the only thing above them was more trail.

Josie's phone had been lodged permanently in hand since the stream, monitoring their movements, a single dot blinking eastbound across a digitized landscape. Neena had pretended not to notice how often Josie checked their progress, despite the path being well trod. Now she wondered if they had both missed something. What if they'd already passed the spring and the fork? The spring was supposed to be small but reliable. But what if it had dried up? Or what if the fork wasn't an obvious split? Even more troubling, if the spring *had* dried up, did that mean they would have to trek all the way back down to the stream to refill? Or could they keep hiking until the next source tomorrow?

Restlessly, they fiddled with the stays and sternum straps—open, closed, up, down—shifting to distribute the weight to their hips and elsewhere—but any relief was temporary.

"Try this," Neena said. With deliberate and mindful footfalls, the earth lent support from beneath. "Walking with a slow roll helps. A little," she added.

"I'm. Already. Doing that."

Neena circled around at the unexpected growl in Josie's throat.

Josie's cheeks were crimson. "Sorry," she grumbled. "These shoes. I don't know how I'm supposed to wear them for two more days."

"We've gotta be close. What does your phone say?"

"I don't know. It says we're in *green.*"

Neena grabbed the map. The dot showed them in the correct area of forest, yet . . . how could they be in the right place, on a straightforward trail, and still feel lost?

Josie swore.

"Calm down," Neena said, instantly regretting it. She handed back the phone. "I'm sure the spring is just ahead."

Calm down? Josie could throttle Neena. The gnarled laurel branches twisted all around them. Her skin was filthy and disgusting, and her braids had frizzed loose. She wasn't even walking anymore—she was hobbling in singular steps. One hobble. Then another. Each brutal motion was a betrayal, her blisters begging her to stop.

"God, I'm starving," Neena whined.

Hunger clawed at Josie, too. A faerie feast shimmered ahead of her, an absurdly long table piled high with silver platters of golden-cooked geese, fruits and breads and butters, cheeses and cakes, tureens of soup and goblets of wine.

Suddenly, Neena stumbled backward to a halt. "Oh, holy—"

Josie almost smashed into her, ripped from dreamland into reality: tufts of mottled fur and blood and viscera, festering black flies and squiggling yellow maggots.

"Ugh." This was muffled by Neena's arm, which covered her mouth and nose.

The smell was horrendous. Josie shielded her airways but couldn't pry away her gaze. A white-tailed deer lay a few feet off trail, its unmoving frame crushing the thick brush. Its eye sockets had been pecked clean, and its muscles were skinny and emaciated. It looked as if it had died of starvation. Scavengers had ripped open the meager carcass, plundering it to expose a grotesque pinwheel of color. Pinks and purples and browns, everything tinged with gray death. Brushed with venous scarlet.

The girls moved along, shaken, but the repulsive stench lingered. Exhaustion plummeted their tanks back to empty. They straggled onward until, at last, Neena crested another slope. "The spring," she said. "I see it! This has to be it."

Water was trickling out of a white PVC pipe that jutted from the earth. Josie had no idea how the system worked, and the spring was minimal and low-flowing, but the water was clear. And it existed. She wanted to weep.

The girls gave feeble hurrahs and exchanged a weak high five.

"Do we refill now?" Neena asked.

Josie's thoughts unclouded enough to form a plan. "Let's find the campsite first, so we can shed our packs."

"Good call. Yes." Neena mumbled it like a zombie. "Shed first. Then filter."

The ground leveled out after the next switchback, and the path forked. The girls released another wilted whoop. Ninety minutes of light remained. Setting up camp would be a hustle—and they were in no condition to hustle—but they were here. They could do it.

Following the Wade Harte to the right, the girls expected to find the Deep Fork clearing after the turn. Instead, they stared into an abyss of more tunnel.

"I guess the clearing isn't *immediately* after the fork?" Neena said.

Josie bit her lip and glanced back behind them. Unsure.

"It's probably just up here." Neena plodded forward with a drained sigh. "I'll keep going, if you want to stay."

But Josie followed. "We're not separating."

Secretly, Neena was relieved. As daylight sank into twilight, she didn't want to be alone, either. The darkness itself didn't frighten her; it was what the darkness concealed. Her brain liked to play tricks. Create specters. She didn't believe in the supernatural, but she did believe in hidden men. Murderers peering in through windows, rapists waiting underneath beds, kidnappers crouched behind closet doors.

When she was young, her brother had turned off the lights while she was fetching a hula hoop from the basement. He'd locked the door and ignored her cries for help, finding her terror to be hilarious. Ma had discovered her an hour later, catatonic on the top step. Darshan wasn't a monster anymore—he was kind and thoughtful, as far from monstrous as possible—but his joke had done permanent damage.

The girls hiked in silence on flat but uneven ground. As the distance from the fork grew, so did Neena's apprehension. "Should we turn around? Try the other path?"

"Win definitely said it was the right fork," Josie said. But she pulled out the printed instructions from Neena's top pouch to confirm. "Yeah. It says right."

"Maybe he remembered wrong. We should have seen the clearing by now."

"He's not wrong," Josie snapped.

The girls stewed in frustrated nervousness. From the forested depths, an owl hooted at the encroaching night.

"Well?" Neena said. "What do you want to do?"

Retracing their steps, they tried the left fork but encountered another compact tunnel. The path was steep and craggy, and, after a few minutes of arduous upward trekking, there was still no clearing. No space anywhere for a tent. The pitch rose in Josie's voice. "Where are we supposed to sleep? We only have an hour of light left."

"I guess we could stretch out our sleeping bags on the trail?"

"On the *trail*? Without a tent?"

"I don't know! I don't want to do that, either." Neena gestured, harassed, in the direction they'd come from, signaling for Josie to turn around.

"You don't think we should look any further up here?" Josie asked.

"I don't know." Neena repeated it, because it was the only true thing. She would have screamed it, if she had the energy. "Do you?"

Josie stared up the trail. Her gaze darkened with unseeing. "Shit," she whispered and then stomped back down.

Neena followed close behind, bumping and dragging her body. She nearly crashed into Josie when Josie stopped abruptly at the fork.

"Now what?" Josie asked.

"Now what *what*?"

"Should we try the other way again? Maybe we didn't walk far enough."

"I still think we should set up camp here at the fork, where there's the most room." Neena imagined them trapped, unprepared, on the trail—pointy black treetops silhouetting themselves against an obsidian sky. "We're running out of time."

"I *know* we're running out of time." Josie shed her pack and scurried up the right path without a goodbye, no longer concerned about being alone. The excruciating rub of inflexible shoes against inflamed flesh fueled her indignation. Neena didn't understand how serious this was. She never took anything seriously.

"Josie," Neena shouted. "Josie!"

"What?"

"Josie!"

As Josie skittered down the mountain, her glasses slid down her nose. She shoved them back up. "*What?*" The question shook with a fury that dissolved the instant she saw.

Neena was holding aside a willowy vine as if it were a theater curtain. The new growth had concealed a third path.

NARROW AND FOOTWORN, the path opened up to a clearing, which was secluded from the main trail inside a dense grove of pine trees. Empty campsites dotted the forest floor. Josie had imagined that Deep Fork would unfurl to reveal a panorama of wide sky and azure mountains. But the clearing remained enclosed. The gap was pretty, at least. Cozy. She stumbled across a blanket of spongy pine needles, her swollen feet already shutting down in anticipation of rest.

"So, the right turn should have been immediately at the fork," Neena was saying. "Instead of taking the right fork and *then* seeing the clearing."

Both girls felt less dumb. Anyone could have made the mistake. The sky hovered on the rim of darkness. Across the gentle slope, seven or eight possibilities spread out before them—flat pockets of uninhabited space, each containing a telltale circle of charred rocks. At the top of the embankment, like a beacon or warning for ships, perched a bright yellow-gold tent. The girls stared at it. The campsite was silent and motionless.

"They're probably still out day hiking," Josie said.

"Or already asleep."

Josie fake-sobbed. "Sleep."

"You know"—Neena glanced again at the yellow-gold disturbance—"if we stay here, we can stop walking."

Josie intuited the rest: *And we can keep our distance from the strangers.* Her pack hit the ground with the weight of a corpse. "Sold."

Neena's pack followed. "Thank God, I don't have to carry that beast again until tomorrow."

Neither girl made an effort to move. Their arms hung flaccid at their sides.

"Refill our water now," Neena asked, "or wait until morning? I'm thinking . . . wait."

Josie's expression hardened into a discouraged scowl. "We *should* do it now, but it's already so dark. And there's so much left to do."

"Try taking off your sunglasses," Neena said.

The sky eased from an ominous dusk into a manageable twilight. Normally, Josie would have laughed, but she was cranky and didn't want to give Neena the satisfaction of being right. "I still think we should wait," she said, wincing onto her knees to rifle through her pack. Travel-size toiletries hurtled to the ground like missiles. "We have less than an hour, and we still have to pitch the tent, start the fire, cook dinner—"

"I wanted to wait, too. I'm not arguing with you." Neena dodged a flattened roll of toilet paper. "Careful."

Locating the case, Josie made the exchange for her regular glasses. The case snapped its impatient jaws shut. As the world sharpened into focus, her anxieties continued in a pile-on. "Hey, did we ever figure out if we're even allowed to have a fire here?" she asked. A campfire would be forbidden the following night in the Misty Rock

Wilderness, but Josie hadn't been able to find any rules about Frazier Mountain.

Neena pointed at the nearby circle of rocks. "All the sites have one of these."

"Yeah, but they aren't using theirs." Josie gestured to the tent up-hill. "Just because campers have done it before, doesn't make it legal."

"Come on, I've never made a fire. It'll complete the experience."

Josie hesitated. Weakened. Caved. "Fine. But if they yell at us, you're the one who has to apologize."

"They're not going to *yell* at us."

Unlike her best friend, Josie was always worried about making other people mad or upset or disappointed. She suppressed it now for the semblance of peace. "Well, if we're building a fire, then there's definitely not enough time for the water—"

"Do you have enough for dinner? For both of us, I mean. I'm pretty low."

Josie still had a full liter of water left. Examining Neena's bottles, she was dismayed to discover that Neena only had a quarter of a liter. She couldn't hold back a sigh. "That's why I told you to go easy earlier."

"Yeah, but we were supposed to have three hours to hang out tonight."

"Well." Josie sighed again. "As long as you're careful, I probably have enough for the both of us."

A moment of testy silence swept over the woods. Then Neena stalked away.

"Where are you going?"

Neena called out without turning around. "To collect sticks for the fire."

"We need to set up the tent first!"

Neena stamped back, grumbling under her breath.

"We've only done it once before." Josie was exasperated. "It would be really hard to put together in the dark."

"Fine. Where is it?"

"It's in my pack, remember?" Josie unzipped her main compartment and yanked out more supplies—first-aid kit, clothing, cook kit, camp chair. The tent was near the bottom, on top of her sleeping bag. Fifteen disgruntled minutes later, they had interlocked the poles and raised the tent, but the process went faster than expected. The girls stared at their red dome, awash with achievement. And then Neena started to wander away.

"We're not done," Josie called after her.

"What?"

"The rainfly." At Neena's blank response, she added, "The part that goes on top of the tent."

Neena appraised the clouds through the pines. "It's not going to rain."

"The weather can change rapidly. All of our shit would get wet."

Neena stomped back, which nettled Josie. It implied that Josie was being a nag, and she was sick of being treated like one. Rained-out gear would ruin their entire trip. And who gave Neena exclusive rights to being miserable? All Josie wanted was to take off her shoes and surrender to the night, but there was work to be done.

The girls pieced together the extra poles and joints and fabric and attached the rainfly over the main dome. Before Neena could think about disappearing again, Josie reminded her that they needed to put together the chairs, too.

"Can't we do that later?" Neena asked.

"No. Let's get it over with."

Josie dumped her chair parts from their pouch as Neena rooted through her pack for her own. Win's girlfriend, Meegan, had purchased the matching pair for his last birthday, but Win had discouraged the girls from bringing both because of the added weight. "One of you can sit on the bear canister," he'd argued. The plastic barrel was approximately the same height as a chair.

Neither girl viewed this as acceptable.

The canister flew out of Neena's pack, along with socks and shirts, a compact stove and fuel, and another sleeping bag. The second pouch was discovered, and then more poles and fabric were flung onto the ground. She jabbed them at each other with livid abandon. Quick to frustration, she threw down the mess. "Fuck you!"

This time, Josie didn't take it personally. It was outrageous how heavy *ultralight* was when you were exhausted. They hadn't practiced putting the chairs together because it had seemed like it would be obvious. Through trial and error, Josie figured out hers while Neena watched and stewed. Then, together, they assembled Neena's.

Josie blinked at their modest creations. "That felt like a microcosm of this whole trip."

"At least we got it right the second time?" Neena framed it as a question. *We* got it wrong the first time. *We* figured it out.

Josie prickled but let it slide, because this three-day trip was about them, plural, together. "Sticks," she instructed. "As many as we can gather."

Neena brightened—somewhat—and hastened into the surrounding woods.

Josie moved with a grimace. Pain bedeviled every step, each one a howling confirmation of the blisters on her heels. On the balls of her feet. On the bony knobs that protruded beside her big toes. They'd been worried about Neena with her borrowed boots, but at least those had already been broken in. Josie shambled around near the campsite, depositing twigs into a pile beside their rock circle. She stole a moment to rest and tidied the rocks, tightening the circle, while Neena dropped off a substantial load of large branches. Fearing a scolding retaliation, Josie limped away for more.

"Did you twist an ankle?" Neena asked. She sounded concerned.

"Blisters."

"Uh-oh."

Josie dismissed it, despite wanting the sympathy. "I'll be fine." Continuing to hobble and gather, she scanned the ground for tracks and scat. She didn't even like bears when they were jailed behind bars in a zoo. The thought of one roving past their tent . . . She tried to recall the scrawled handwriting on the plywood notice board. Had any of those hikers spotted a bear at Deep Fork? She couldn't remember, but surely it would have jumped out at her at the time.

Neena dropped another armful onto the pile. It landed with a satisfying clatter. It seemed like enough to start the fire, so they tossed the heftiest branches into the pit.

Josie packed some of the smaller sticks in between. "Kindling, I think?"

Neena shrugged. "That sounds right."

Searching and collecting had eased the tension between them. Josie found the matches, and they took turns trying to light the kindling. A few twigs singed, but none would burn. Their frustration rose again. Now that they'd stopped moving, the chill from the lofty elevation crawled under Josie's skin. It settled into her bones.

She shivered. "I'm gonna get my hoodie. Would you like yours?"

Glowering at the matches, Neena shook her head. She still looked warm and flush. Her body temperature was always higher than Josie's. Josie located her own hoodie on the ground beside her pack and brushed off a stray pine needle, faintly tacky with sap. Zipping up, she spotted a new hole in the stitching where the left sleeve met the left shoulder. Holes tattered the elbows, too, in a way that seemed cool and purposeful. Like she didn't give a damn.

Josie did give a damn, and she would have preferred a new hoodie, but it never felt okay to buy one when there were other things she needed more.

Something else on the ground caught her eye. She carried it over. Neena was confused. "You want to burn your journal?"

"Only a few sheets," Josie said. "The paper will catch fire, and maybe that'll be enough to get the rest going."

Win had said it was a bad idea to bring their journals—again, the unnecessary weight—*Write on the backs of the printouts, if you're that desperate*—but the girls couldn't imagine not having the option. Finally, they felt vindicated to have ignored his advice. Josie tore out two sheets, crumpled them up, and tucked them into the kindling. The paper lit. The burn was quick, but the paper slid the fire onto a skinny twig.

Josie sucked in her breath. "Come on," she begged the other sticks.

The fire went out.

"Try it again," Neena said, growing excited. They tore and tucked another sheet. "Do you think we're supposed to blow on it?" she asked. "To give it more oxygen?"

"We breathe in oxygen. We breathe out carbon dioxide."

"But doesn't fire need air or whatever? Isn't that a thing?"

"Yeah, but it's too small. We'd blow it out."

Neena leaned into the circle and started puffing anyway.

"You're going to blow it out!" Josie said.

Another puff. "No, it's like a bellows."

"A what?"

"Those old-timey, squeezey accordion things. Like in Victorian times— Aha!"

Orange flames spread across a second stick and then licked onto a third. Above the kindling, a stout branch sputtered, thinking of catching fire. As more sticks were thrust at the blaze, the girls learned that dry sticks worked better than damp, and, at last, the campfire roared into life. They were as proud as cavewomen.

They were also paranoid about it dying again. "You watch the fire and start dinner," Neena said. "I'll collect more wood, so you don't have to walk."

It felt generous. As if Josie had expected Neena to have either forgotten about her feet or to not care, even though Neena wasn't that type of person. Neena had never been either absentminded or malicious. Guilt rumbled inside Josie.

The sun had set, and the light was dying. They strapped on their headlamps before separating. If their emotions hadn't been stretched so thin, they might have laughed at the sight—the white spot in the center of their foreheads like a blinding third eye. Josie used hers to spelunk inside the bear canister. The barrel had a tight screw-on lid and notches around the sides, a design that prevented bears from unscrewing it and getting the goodies inside. It held all their food. And, hopefully, it also held all of the enticing, food-related smells.

Tonight's dinner was lamb curry with rice, courtesy of Dr. Chandrasekhar. All Josie had to do was reheat it. She was surprised to locate it inside a bulky glass mason jar. Unlike Win, Neena's mom had forgotten they'd be carrying everything on their backs. Josie dumped the contents into a tiny pot before realizing the stove wasn't ready. As she threaded the collapsible stove onto its fuel canister, the campfire dimmed. Inside her vault of fading memories, the shadow of her father poked expertly at a fire with a stick. Beside the woodpile was a long, sturdy branch they'd rejected for being too damp. Josie picked it up and poked. A gratifying shower of sparks exploded into the night sky.

From the depths of the forest, Neena whooped.

Josie smiled. She developed a routine—darting back and forth between preparing the curry and tending to the fire. It was nerve-wracking how quickly the flames wanted to die out, and it seemed silly to use the stove when they already had a fire. But to use the fire, they would have also needed a grill to lay across the rocks.

It was ridiculous how much gear was required for roughing it.

The sensation of falling light barely lingered on the fringes of Deep Fork, just beyond their shelter of pines. Neena's headlamp bobbed like a lantern through the dark and quiet trees. Periodically she would stop to unload another bundle of sticks.

"That smells good," she said on her final deposit.

Josie glowed in agreement. The little stove hissed, sending up threads of rising smoke. After dividing their dinner between two bowls, she lowered herself into a chair, closed her eyes, and groaned. Neena chorused beside her.

"I am never getting up," Josie said.

"Mmm," Neena said in agreement.

The girls ate ravenously, teeth and tongues and fingers and sporks. Every scrap was devoured. Neena's parents were from Kolkata, and her mother's Bengali cooking had been keeping Josie fed for years. She loved it. The pleasurable tear of tender meat, the nutty tang from the mustard seeds, the warming heat from the green chilis. Normally, she would have killed for a side of chapati, but she was so famished that flatbread didn't matter. Lamb curry had never tasted so delectable.

The remaining water was wedged between their chairs, and Josie reached down for a sip. Neena was already glugging from the bottle.

"Hey," Josie said.

Neena's body slunk like guilty dog. She handed it over. "I know, I know."

The water was tepid but refreshing. Josie drank mindfully. They needed enough to wash the dishes and brush their teeth—with an emergency ration still left over at bedtime.

Neena's headlamp vanished with a faint tick. Feeling for the rubber button, Josie clicked hers off, too. Absolute night cloaked the forest. The cool mountain air smelled like woodsmoke and evergreens. Josie inhaled deeply. Her body grew heavy and relaxed. Her gaze zoned out, inert, at the fire. The flames crackled, hot and hypnotic. Smoke billowed in phantasmagoric shrouds.

"We did it," Neena said after several minutes. Her voice was thick and slow.

"Yep. We did."

"One day down. Two to go."

Josie managed to laugh. So did Neena. They lacked the energy to set their empty bowls on the ground. The insects chirred, the fire spit.

Josie bit her lip. "Are you worried about tomorrow?"

"Nah. We've got this." Neena hoped she sounded reassuring, but undercut her own confidence a few beats later. "At least it's not uphill. That was the worst part."

"Definitely."

"And our return on Wednesday will be downhill."

"*Wednesday.*"

The word enveloped Neena in the same melancholia. Wednesday meant the end. "Hump Day," she trilled, because it was such an odious phrase.

But Josie didn't laugh. The mood didn't lighten.

"It sucks that we're so close to the summit, but we won't even get to see it," Josie said. The top of Frazier Mountain was only a mile and a half away, but the trail to reach it was separate from the Wade Harte.

Neena frowned into the snickering fire. Still wanting to help. "Maybe we could hit it on the way back. We could stash our packs here so the climb wouldn't be so bad."

"Maybe that's what the other campers did."

Though they hadn't discussed them since arriving at the campsite, Neena and Josie remained keenly aware of their neighbors. Neighbor? Simultaneously, the girls wondered if the other tent belonged to one person or two. They glanced up the slope, but the pitch black had long since swallowed the yellow gold.

An earsplitting crack exploded across the clearing.

The girls jumped and shrieked, but it was only the fire. They glanced at each other and finally started laughing again, punchy and shaken and tired. Their former classmates would have been partying by now, swapping ghost stories and urban legends. Or was that only kids' stuff? Josie supposed they'd be drinking beer and smoking weed, but she had a better idea. She revealed a small Ziploc packed with something else entirely.

Neena perked up. "Marshmallows! I thought—"

"I refuse to let you move away without tasting a proper s'more."

The ingredients were yet another thing Win had told them not to bring, which Josie had ignored to the detriment of her own back. But it was criminal that Neena had only ever made s'mores in a microwave. She tossed the bag to Neena and followed it with a bar of dark chocolate. The graham crackers had been padded inside a shirt to prevent breakage. Josie selected two sticks of scrubby underbrush from the reject pile, lounged back into her seat, and held a skewered marshmallow toward the fire.

"I like mine nearly burnt," she said.

"You're the best," Neena said. "I thought we were going without dessert tonight."

"Bite your tongue."

After a leisurely minute toasting the sugary pillows, Neena's forehead creased. "So . . . remind me. How does the chocolate melt?"

Josie's brow folded into an identical frown. Years had passed since she'd made a s'more, and it had been with her parents' help. "Huh."

"Do we cook it on a separate stick?"

That didn't seem right, but Josie couldn't think of another way. She held Neena's stick while Neena procured two more, pronged this time. Balancing the graham crackers on the pronged ends, the girls topped each with a square of chocolate. Immediately, Josie's dropped into the fire. They erupted with more laughter, and she tried again, concentrating on steadying her exhausted arms.

Again into the fire. Their laughter grew loose and giggly.

Neena examined her chocolate, which had scarcely melted, and her marshmallow, which was golden brown. "Screw it. I'm going in." She made a sandwich and took a bite. Her eyes closed with hedonistic delight. "Yes," she said through a stuffed, sticky mouth. *Yeth.* "Oh!" Her eyes leapt open in surprise. "The chocolate is melting from the heat of the marshmallow."

Tears of laughter pricked Josie's eyes as she motioned toward the pronged stick. "I knew this was too hard."

"I bet milk chocolate would melt even faster."

"I actually remembered my dad using milk chocolate, but I brought dark—"

"Because dark is better."

"Exactly. Sorry."

"Don't be. I love it. My first proper s'more!" Neena's shout reverberated throughout the forest, and Josie admonished her, still giggling. Like the boy earlier on the trail, Neena adopted the voice of a hackneyed redneck. "Quit yer worrying, girl. Ain't nobody gonna hear us, not all the way out—"

She cut herself off. Her eyes darted to the woods.

Josie's spine froze along its full length. The fire popped. Insects rattled. Josie glanced at Neena—overly stiff and riveted to the tree line—and then flopped back into her seat. Flush with embarrassment, she tried to hide her anger. "Ha ha."

Without detaching her gaze, Neena lowered her voice. "Something is out there."

"Smokey, right? Ooh, or is it Brother Bear?"

"Shh!"

The shush was piercing. Josie's sinews tightened. Neena nodded toward the darkness ahead of them. "What is it?" Josie whispered.

"I don't know. Something . . . large."

They listened. Waited. With a thumping chest, Josie silently set down her twig. The burning marshmallow sank into the pine needles. Her hands gripped onto each other, her knuckles whitened. She twisted her stone ring.

Neena's eyes widened with terror. "There!"

"Where?" Josie hissed.

"You didn't hear that?"

Josie turned frantic. "Hear what? What is it?"

"There. There it is again!" Neena bolted up. Her chair tipped backward and clashed to the forest floor. "Oh my God! Oh my God!"

Josie vaulted to her feet, hands clawing for Neena. She screamed.

"OW," NEENA SAID, prying Josie's fingers from her arm.

Confusion flickered within Josie's dilated pupils as Neena burst into cackling laughter. Stunned, Josie was forced to reorient herself. Outrage swiftly replaced fright. "I knew it. I knew it!" Humiliation scorched Josie's cheeks. "God, you're such a bitch. Why do you always do that? When are you gonna learn shit like that isn't funny?"

"Oh, come on. That was pretty funny."

"No. It wasn't. There *really are* things out there, and we're alone. In the middle of nowhere."

Neena's tone corroded with derision. "Not the bears again."

"I'm not making them up! They fucking live out here!"

"Yeah, and your yelling is scaring them all away." The instant it left her mouth, Neena wished she could take it back. She knew she shouldn't have tricked Josie even before she'd done it. But now she was already caught in the loop. "I don't know why you're so scared of them, anyway, when it's people you should be worried about."

"Do you see any other people around here?"

"Do you see any bears?"

Tears sprung to Josie's eyes. She fought them. "Fuck you."

"I'm just saying—"

"Maybe I *should* be afraid of people. Maybe I should be afraid of *you*. It's not like mass shooters hang out in the woods." Josie spread her arms in a wide and fuming gesture. "No masses."

Neena shoved the barb aside. "I'm not talking about mass shooters. I'm talking about serial killers."

"Please." Josie stomped toward her pack. "Son of Sam, Zodiac, the Osborne Slayer—yeah, they're all hiding out there, waiting to get us. Should I also be worried about the Slender Man or some other creepypasta bullshit? What about that guy with the hook?"

"Actually . . ." Neena said, her inner voice battling with itself, pleading that she didn't have to prove her point. Shouting that it would be cruel to force any more horrific stories into Josie's head. "Tons of crimes have been committed in national forests. Cary Stayner in Yosemite. David Carpenter, the Trailside Killer." The examples burst forth, unwanted, like pop-up ads. Neena's father was a lawyer who investigated claims of innocence for wrongful conviction cases. Neena knew a lot about the worst humanity had to offer. "Israel Keyes. That guy was really messed up. He hid kill kits in rural areas all across the country—"

"I don't want to know—"

"Gary Michael Hilton! They literally called him the National Forest Serial Killer. When we were kids, he killed a man and woman right here in Pisgah, right in this area—"

"Why would you tell me this?"

"He's in prison now, but do you remember that group of hikers who went missing a couple of years ago near Hot Springs? Two girls and a guy. They were found murdered only a week later." Hot Springs was a rural town located in a distant area of Pisgah. It wasn't close enough to be a concern, but it was close enough for Neena to make her point. "The guy's body was untouched, but the girls had rope burns around their wrists and ankles."

Josie looked up from digging through her pack. The shovel was clenched in her hand. "*Four* hikers went missing." Win and his friends had volunteered in the massive search party. "The other boyfriend was never found, and they think he's still on the run. The crime was personal. Not random. And I don't want to talk about this anymore."

"I'm just saying—"

"Fine. Enough." Josie was crying as she fled away, gait limping, with the shovel and a handful of toilet paper. "Are you happy now?"

No, Neena wasn't happy.

The moon was sliced neatly down the center, half in darkness, half in light. It was close, and it blotted out any additional starlight that she had been expecting. No more glimmered here than what she might have seen in her own backyard. Perhaps they were still too close to Asheville's electric glow. But this place didn't look like home as Josie's headlamp switched on and teetered between the skeletal shadows of pines.

Neena shuddered. Maybe it had been easier to attack Josie's weaknesses than to face her own. But just because Neena didn't like the darkness didn't mean she couldn't handle it. She grabbed a sanitary pad and some toilet paper from the smushed roll and then shuffled off in the opposite direction. Not wanting another scolding, she made sure to walk far enough away from their tent. According to Josie, the scent of urine appealed to bears because it carried the smell of whatever food the human had recently eaten.

The ground crunched underneath her boots. Neena's lamp only illuminated enough to see one step at a time. The unlit woods meant that the summer fireflies—the only cheerful denizens of the night— were already gone for the season. But, away from the campfire, the mosquitos thickened. She swatted them sightlessly into her bare arms.

The missing and murderous boyfriend lurched into her mind. Until Josie had mentioned him, Neena had forgotten that he was a part of the story, but now it was easy to imagine him hiking south into these woods. She had to remind herself how unlikely that actually was. No doubt he'd hitched a ride somewhere or was hiding out at a friend's house. Or was still hiding up near Hot Springs. Why hadn't she been able to stop herself from trying to scare Josie? She had only angered Josie, and she had scared herself, instead. Her muscles ached as badly as her conscience.

At least she still didn't need the shovel. Not yet.

After finishing, Neena returned to the fire. It had already weakened in the short time since they'd stopped feeding it. She burned the toilet paper and debated tossing the bloodied pad into the low flames with it, but the material was probably plastic or something awful like that, so she stuffed it into the trash bag inside the bear canister.

The cold night slithered over her. She rubbed her itchy, bitten arms and leaned toward the waning heat. The pit belched out a caustic cloud. Eyes stinging, she gasped soundlessly, determined not to alert Josie to her mistake. Josie would know better than to stick her face into the smoke. Neena blinked through the rush of tears.

Where *was* Josie? She strained to hear the shovel against earth.

The fire crackled and snapped.

"Josie?" she called out.

She waited a few seconds.

"Josie?" Her voice rose. "Is everything okay?"

Neena dabbed at her burning eyes with her shirtsleeve, which was salty and stiff from dried sweat. Fear gnawed. She couldn't see Josie's headlamp. What if, in her anger, Josie had walked too far? What if she was lost? All Neena knew about getting lost in the woods was that you were supposed to stay put until someone found you. Her parents had told her that when she was a child. But did the same strategy apply to adults? They had packed an emergency whistle, but Neena doubted Josie had taken it with her. Should she rouse the strangers in the yellow-gold tent to help her search? What if the murderous boyfriend was out there? What if he was in the tent?

She yelled Josie's name again.

"Yeah?" a distant voice called back.

Neena's arms curled around her stomach. She felt embarrassed at how quick she'd been to panic. A lamp bobbed into view. It approached slowly, bumpily, through the dark forest. Like being blinded by an oncoming car's brights, she couldn't see Josie herself until she finally stepped into the firelight. She looked broken. Depleted.

"I thought you were lost," Neena said.

Josie tossed the shovel to the ground. "No."

Worried that it might have sounded like she was suggesting a flaw in Josie's navigational skills, Neena lied. "I got turned around out there, too. How are your feet doing?"

Josie gave a morose shrug but then sharpened with an accusatory thought. "Did you remember to bury—"

"I burned it. And I put the pad in the trash."

"Ugh, that reminds me. We need to get rid of the canister."

"No problem," Neena said. But as she tried to add their empty bowls to the canister, Josie harped again.

"You have to wash them off first."

"I thought we were running low on water."

"Yeah, but we still have to wash them off. They'll get gross. That's one of the reasons why I wanted you to be careful with the water."

Neena swallowed her irritation because she was still paying penance. They poured a splash of water into each bowl and scrubbed them with their sporks. When Josie grew agitated that hers wasn't spotless, Neena physically removed it from her hands. "It's fine,"

Neena said, packing away the dishes and screwing the lid shut. "Good enough."

Expecting Josie to snap back, Neena felt even worse when Josie remained silent. On the ground between them lay the remnants of Josie's s'more. The shame sunk in deeper. With a timid voice, Neena asked, "Would you like a new one?"

Josie broke off the stick ends that had touched the food and tossed them into the fire. "No," she said. The graham cracker, chocolate square, and marshmallow followed.

The flames burned and swallowed them.

Neena slunk away with the canister, which had to be placed far from their tent for safety. At least it wasn't a bear bag, which she would have had to hoist into a tree. She had no idea how she would have managed that alone.

"Wait!" Josie said. "Our toiletries."

Everything that smelled had to be stored away. The girls brushed their teeth and then spit into the final dregs of the fire. Only embers remained, pulsing lumps of orange and red. Neena wished she could rinse out her mouth, but she didn't dare touch the water.

The girls rifled through their belongings for any remaining scented items—sunscreen, baby wipes. "Lip balm?" Josie asked, uncapping it to sniff.

Neena shrugged.

It all went in.

"Make sure you take it far from the tent," Josie reminded her.

Neena lugged away the unwieldy canister. Though she didn't have any blisters, her feet were still killing her. Her body was still freezing. Without the campfire, the temperature had taken another significant drop.

A jagged tree root snagged her boot. She nearly face-planted, and the canister thudded to the ground. Struggling up, she brushed the grit from her palms. The woods were as black as crow wings. Feathery shadows shifted. Sentient trees concealed. Her imagination began to spin wild and nightmarish tales, and she ditched the canister.

Back at the campsite, Josie was unfurling her sleeping bag inside the tent. "Everything go okay?"

"Fine," Neena said icily.

"I didn't know what to do with our packs, so I brought them in. I don't know. It seemed . . . vulnerable to leave them out there."

"That's fine," Neena said again, ducking to enter. The backpacks overcrowded the cramped space, but she agreed that it felt safer to keep them close.

The wind whistled across the netting. Josie poked her head through the flaps and made an ugly noise. Neena didn't ask. She waited to be told. As Josie turned toward her, their white headlamps bore directly into each other's eyes. They both hissed as if being attacked and winced away.

"The embers are still smoldering," Josie said.

"Is that a problem?"

"We have to put them out completely. Something could spark and catch fire."

"So put them out."

"I already took off my shoes."

Neena wanted to take off *her* shoes, too. She wanted to burrow into Win's stupid girlfriend's stupid sleeping bag and not speak to Josie again until morning—until their emotions had chilled and their bodies were in less pain. She huffed outside, back into the cold. The fire had been threatening to die out the entire time, but now it was impossible to fully extinguish. She was too afraid to stomp on it, blowing made it worse, and spitting wasn't enough. The embers clung on for dear life. Her teeth chattered. Stretching her upper half back into the tent, she searched for, and nabbed, the water bottle.

"Hey," Josie said as she realized what was happening.

The embers extinguished with a satisfying sizzle.

"What the fuck!" Josie shouted.

"I put the fire out."

"You don't use *water*."

"What do you mean, you don't use *water*?" Neena emphasized it in the same snotty way. "I'm pretty sure firemen aren't shooting Cheerwine from their hoses."

Josie's tone clenched. "I meant that everybody knows you smother a campfire with dirt to save water. And that was the last of what I'd saved."

"*Everybody knows?* Jesus, Josie." Reentering, Neena jerkily zipped up the solid flap behind her, then the netting flap. Woodsmoke choked the tent. It permeated their clothing, hair, skin, lips. They tasted it on their tongues.

They didn't speak as Neena wrestled with her sleeping bag. Their headlamps shone on opposite corners of the tent. Backs to each other, they removed their bras through the armholes of their shirts. Neena unlaced her boots and stifled a moan. The unwanted brutes were discarded at the end of her sleeping bag, away from her head so that she wouldn't have to smell them. Her feet had never felt so sore—or so blissfully free. She exchanged her soiled socks for clean ones and put on her hoodie.

Josie, who was cold-natured, removed her jeans to add a pair of long johns and then wriggled back into the jeans. She also added a second pair of socks and a knitted hat, as well as a long-sleeved shirt between her T-shirt and hoodie.

You are going to boil, Neena thought with exhilarating meanness.

The girls both stormed into their downy sleeping bags—as best they could storm in an overstuffed, two-person tent—and turned off their lamps. Darkness engulfed them.

"Shit," Neena mumbled. Realizing she didn't have a pillow.

Josie did not respond.

They had planned to use their clothing for pillows, but the only thing Neena could locate in the dark was a clean T-shirt. She tucked it underneath her head. The comfort was flat and unsatisfying. Knowing Josie, she probably had an amazing pillow. She'd probably made it while Neena was snuffing out the fire.

"All I meant," Josie said, her voice slicing through the dark, "was that you never know what might happen, and water is kinda important. The *most* important, actually."

Neena closed her eyes and hoped that Josie would choke on her self-righteousness.

"Like, what if we try the water filter at the spring tomorrow, and it doesn't work?" Josie pressed.

"Then I suppose we'll have a shitty morning as we walk back to my car."

"Or what if one of us gets thirsty in the middle of the night?"

"I told you I'm sorry." She had not. "Okay? It won't happen again."

Silence. Twenty seconds, maybe.

"It's just . . . sometimes I think you don't take me seriously. It's not outlandish to want to save a little water in case of an emergency."

"Oh my God, Josie. How many times do you want me to apologize?"

"*Once* would be nice, but I'm not asking for that. I'm tired of you making me feel like shit all the time over totally rational things."

Neena was blindsided. "Excuse me?"

"It's not unreasonable for me to want water, or to want the tent set up before sundown, or to be afraid of animals that can eat me. It's common. Fucking. Sense."

"Okay." Neena inhaled. Her lungs filled to capacity. "You want to play this game, let's play it. How about how shitty you've made *me* feel today? 'It's common fucking sense.' Well, I'm sorry I've never been in the goddamn fucking woods before. And it's not common sense. Somebody told you once, too, so you don't have to condescend to me like I'm an idiot every time I do something wrong—"

"*Me?* You're the one—"

"I'm the one holding your hand." Neena unleashed her resentment. She snarled it. "Without me, you wouldn't even be here. You'd still be at home, feeling sorry for yourself like always."

Josie's voice glinted into a blade. "Without *me*, we wouldn't be here. I'm the one who found the trail, I'm the one who had the gear—"

"Your brother found the trail, and your brother had the gear. And you lean on him like you lean on me. God, I'm so sick of it! Always having to make the decisions for both of us. Always having to watch what I say around you."

"Are you serious? This is you watching what you say around me?"

"Oh, please. The moment I mention Los Angeles—"

There was a sharp intake from Josie.

"—or college anymore, you freak out. I'm moving in five days, and I'm terrified, and I can't even talk about it with my best friend because she gets mad at me. Because, somehow, her feelings on the subject are more valid than mine. Her feelings always win."

"Well, I'm sorry that it's hard for me to pity someone who's going to an awesome school in an awesome city." Josie pronounced the word "awesome" as if it tasted like dung. "I'm sorry that it's hard to have two supportive parents and that your life is so perfect and easy."

"That's not fair—"

"What's not fair is that we made the same fucking As, and you get to follow your dreams, and I get to keep working at Kmart. So, yeah." Josie spat it. "Maybe I'm testy."

"All I'm saying is that I wish you could separate the two things and be happy for me. Or at least accept that I might be scared right now, too. But instead, you keep dragging me down—"

"Dragging you down?"

"Yes!" Neena hated how shrill her tone had become.

"How can I drag you down when nothing can stop you? You never stop needling. You *never* know when to quit."

"Because if I didn't push you, you'd never do anything! You'd be just like your mom."

There was a ghastly beat. The tent thickened with malevolence, and Josie's voice shaped into a damning and unrecognizable form. "You're selfish, you're reckless, and you have no idea what you're talking about."

Both girls burst into tears.

DEEP DOWN SOUTH in the Appalachian Mountain system, in the Blue Ridge province, in the Pisgah National Forest, in the narrow gap between Frazier Mountain and the Misty Rock Wilderness, sat a tent. Tucked inside its fragile shell, two teenage girls were crying in the dark. Their tears streamed hot and quiet, punctuated by sniffles. Blubbery snot was gulped and choked. The girls lay side by side. Back to back. Their sleeping bags touched, but they had never been farther apart.

Me, me, me.

You, you, you.

Their unspoken, unscreamed grievances had finally exploded, and neither girl understood why she hadn't been able to back down. Or laugh it off. Or attempt to salvage whatever was left. But perhaps it was easier to attack and sever ties now than to watch their friendship disintegrate over time as they grew into their new and separate adulthoods. Perhaps it was easier to kill something than to save it.

The tent bottom was nothing more than a tarp. They'd been

advised to bring sleeping pads, which would have provided an additional barrier of insulation and cushioning from the ground, but they had decided not to. They'd needed the room for their chocolate and marshmallows, for their chairs and journals. Cold dampness seeped up through the crinkly fabric. Brittle pine needles stabbed and hard rocks wedged, agitating and deepening their bruises. Ironically, journaling might have provided some comfort.

Neither girl was willing to turn on a light.

Outside the tent, a lone bird called in the night.

Nothing responded.

Hours passed.

Every speck and seedling that landed against the nylon, every leaf and stick that tumbled over the earth, was thunderous and abrasive. To Neena, the wind blowing through the trees sounded like rushing vehicles. It reminded her of walking across an overpass in a big city. It made her anxious, like the guardrail was broken and she was about to fall.

To Josie, the wind sounded like the ocean. It reminded her of her father's arms, strong and hairy and tanned. Every August, her family used to rent a house on Folly Beach, where they would spend a whole week gorging on shrimp burgers and basking in the sun. In an alternate timeline, she would have been there right now—or maybe returning home, asleep in the back seat with Win, sand on their flip-flops. But the tradition had died with her father.

Grief was peculiar. Enough time had passed that she was okay, mostly. Days or even weeks could go by without incident. But then something unexpected would happen, and the pain would come roaring back. The something could be good or bad. The response was simply triggered by being caught *unaware*. Her hurt was still instantly accessible. Her membranes were still thin and defenseless.

She was roasting in her sleeping bag. Silently, she stripped off her hat and the extra pair of socks. Her arms throbbed with the prickling heat of sunburnt skin. She imagined her father surrounded by nothing. She imagined herself, on the other side of nothing, surrounded by too much and not enough.

Josie was sweating.

Suffocating.

Neena was freezing. Shivering and shaking, she hated herself for not bringing more layers, and she hated Josie even more for bringing plenty. How could summer feel so much like winter? She had a headache from crying and a mounting pressure in her intestines. She tried to ignore it. All she wanted was to sleep soundly and without dreams.

It was so cold outside. So dark.

Neena had glow-in-the-dark stars on her bedroom ceiling. Her family—and even Josie—believed they were decorative, but they actually functioned as nightlights. Their soft green luminescence comforted and lulled her to sleep. There would be no such solace here. Rustling leaves gave the impression of a black bear trundling through the woods. Had she dropped the canister far enough away? The question made her molars grind.

Her stomach gurgled. Unable to wait a second longer, Neena squirmed out of her sleeping bag. Any last vestiges of warmth vanished. Her eyes had adjusted enough that she could see her boots, but her hands were so numb that it was difficult to tie the laces.

Beside her, Josie was stiff with alertness.

Neena grabbed a few squares of toilet paper and shoved them into a pocket, but she couldn't find the shovel and didn't want to ask. She groped for the exit. The zippers shrieked. She winced, even though Josie was already awake. Even though she wanted to propel Josie off the side of the mountain.

Josie's sleeping bag swished as she lifted her head. An inquiry.

"I have to pee," Neena whispered in annoyance, and as the flaps fell back behind her, she turned on her headlamp.

Mist had spread across the entirety of Deep Fork. The air shimmered in the lamplight. A screech owl called out to her solitary beam, its strange hoot like the whinny of a horse. With a shudder, Neena stumbled forward into the misty pines. Water steeped through the threads of her clothing. It dampened her nose and cheeks. Cautiously, she trod, aiming for the same area that she had used earlier, trying to fight the sensation of being watched by someone or something lurking just out of sight.

Her lamp ran into a thicket.

She didn't remember one being here. Deciding that she'd steered too far to the left, she retraced her steps, back and diagonally to the right, but then hit another thicket.

Too far to the right or not enough?

Her light scanned the thickening mist. It was impossible to see more than a few feet ahead. She didn't know where she was, but she had to go. Scouring the ground, she located a rock to use for digging. It was glacial to the touch. Neena tugged her sleeves down over her hands and clumsily held on to it through her hoodie. When the hole seemed deep enough, she undid her jeans. The air was an icy slap against her skin.

For as long as I live, she vowed, *I will never go camping again.*

Business done and wiped, she reached for her pants. A faint crack rang out from beyond the thicket—the sound of a twig snapping.

Neena froze.

It's nothing, she thought.

But then another twig snapped.

Her chest seized. Frantically, she hunted for the source, but the mist had swollen into a fog. Everything was the same color of wet darkness.

Something was moving. The forest was disturbed. Though the movements felt predatory, Neena didn't think the something was an animal. She fumbled to switch off her headlamp. Anybody out there might see her light, panning back and forth, and know she was lost. A mosquito whined in her ear. Startled, she crushed it, smearing her lobe with her own blood.

She waited.

Listened.

The rustling and crunching grew louder. Closer. It wasn't her imagination. Still in a crouch, Neena's legs began to shake. Goose bumps dimpled her bottom and lower back. Never before had her flesh been so vulnerable or exposed.

The noises honed into distinctly human footsteps.

Fear thumped through her. The footsteps moved heavily, steadily through the underbrush. Her vision strained. They were only a few feet away, but she couldn't see anything through the veil of fog. She prayed her light hadn't been noticed.

On the other side of the thicket, they stopped.

She covered her mouth. Positive her breathing was audible.

Solid and immovable as a boulder, the presence felt menacing. A darkness darker than the surrounding forest, a mass as obliterating as a black hole. Every fear she had ever had of the night, compacted and concentrated into a single, unseen form.

But then, just as unexpectedly, the footsteps moved on. Heavily, steadily. Fainter and fainter, until they faded away altogether. The woods held their secret in silence.

Neena's limbs weakened into jelly, and she sank toward the forest floor. She hastily rose to avoid falling into her own excrement. Fumbling, she pulled up her jeans, used her boot to swipe the dirt back over the hole, and reexamined her surroundings.

She had no idea where the tent was. Her mind hurtled through the options. She'd left the emergency whistle in the tent—*stupid, stupid*—but if she cried out, Josie would come. Probably. But who *else* might come? Though Neena couldn't hear the footsteps anymore, surely their owner was still close enough to hear if she called for help.

The tent had to be nearby. She hadn't walked that far. Had she?

Why didn't she bring a compass? She could have navigated by the stars or some shit! Okay, no. That wasn't true. But she couldn't stay here, and she couldn't risk using her headlamp, either.

Neena hunched over and crept along the thicket line. Her best guess was that when the bushes ended, the tent would be at about forty-five degrees.

If she was remembering the correct thicket.

If she was oriented in the correct direction.

How easy it would be to wander in the *wrong* direction.

With each step, she tested the ground with a toe before putting down the entire boot. The pine-needle carpet crackled softly—still too loudly—beneath her feet. Her fingers felt the thicket's end before she saw it. She took a frightened and hesitant step away from the vegetation, her hand dislodged . . . and she was unmoored.

Fog rolled around the pines like a current as Neena waded into the dark sea. She swam between the trees, arms outstretched, hands grasping at nothing. She shuffled forward in meek increments. Each time she moved, the other footsteps moved, too. The sound was in her head. It wasn't real. Was she alone or had they returned?

Panic screamed at her to run, but she fought it, afraid of alerting the stranger to her location, afraid of running in the wrong direction, afraid, afraid, afraid—

Her toe tapped against a low stone. The rest of her boot came down with confidence, but another stone was touching it, and the rocks clattered together. Startled, Neena tripped over a third rock, kicking it, only to realize she was standing inside the campfire circle. She shot off and sprinted several feet, expecting to crash into the tent.

All she found was more fog.

"Neena?"

Neena darted toward the familiar voice. Her outstretched hands smacked into nylon. Scrabbling for the door flaps, she lunged inside and feverishly zipped them closed behind her. "Somebody is out there," she hissed.

Josie didn't respond.

"There were footsteps."

"Yeah," Josie said at a regular volume. She was fuming. "Yours. That's why I called out."

"Shh!"

"Seriously?" The question wasn't, *Are you being serious?* But, *Are you seriously kidding me with this same fucking joke?* Neena wrapped a hand over Josie's mouth, and Josie let out a muffled cry. The force of Neena's pounding heart against Josie's back made Josie stiffen in alarm. She fell quiet. Neena released her.

The girls sat—almost touching—in petrified silence.

Their ears strained. *Wind. Insects. Leaves.* As the seconds ticked into a minute, Josie shoved Neena away, incensed.

"I swear," Neena said, still whispering, "somebody was out there."

Josie flumped noisily back into bed. "It's not even warm anymore," she grouched, meaning her sleeping bag.

"I *swear*," Neena said.

Perhaps it was the note of desperation that gave Josie pause. Finally, she lowered her voice to match. "Are you sure it wasn't a deer?"

"No. It was a person."

Josie remained skeptical. "I bet it was a deer."

"It wasn't . . ." Neena said through clenched teeth, ". . . a deer." Now that the threat had seemingly passed, anger rushed back in. She yanked off her boots and crawled into her sleeping bag. "And it wasn't a bear, either."

The silence was hostile but brief.

"Okay, then you probably heard the person from the other tent." Even though Josie was humoring the idea, her tone was frosty. "And you probably freaked them out as much as they freaked you out."

Neena seethed because the explanation made sense. Hell, maybe Josie's first guess was correct, and it was a stupid deer, and her imagination had gotten carried away in the fog. What did a deer sound like, anyway? Or maybe it was an elk. What *was* an elk? Was it just a larger kind of deer? She hated how ignorant this trip made her feel.

The temperature continued to drop, and Neena shivered in her wet clothing. Fog had saturated the cotton, refusing to let it dry. Until now, she'd never understood the purpose of wicking fabrics. It seemed against common sense that a synthetic would dry faster than a natural fiber, but, clearly, she was wrong again.

A rock underneath the tarp jammed into her hips. Her useless T-shirt pillow made her neck crooked with knots. Her head still throbbed from the crying headache.

It wasn't a deer.

Two faces materialized in her mind: the young teenage girls who had been found murdered on a hiking trail a few years ago in

Indiana. One of the girls had managed to use her phone to secretly record audio and video of the man that police believed to be their killer. The news story had been chilling—the idea that you could be out with your best friend, doing something as basic as taking a stroll through the woods, with no idea of what was waiting for you on the other side of the bend.

The fog curled around the tent like the tail of a sleeping wolf.

Her thoughts drifted to the fourth hiker here in Pisgah, the one suspected of murdering his friends in Hot Springs. The one still on the lam. Earlier that day, the boy on the trail who had reminded her of Win had teased them about a man who raided these campsites at night, but . . . sometimes jokes were based on rumors. And sometimes rumors were based on truth.

Nobody is out to get me.

The fog nudged and bumped against the tent.

Nature isn't out to get me.

The fog was merely a low-lying cloud that had rolled in. This was a normal meteorological phenomenon that happened in the mountains. *I'm falling asleep on a cloud*, she tried to convince herself, *and it's idyllic.*

I'm falling asleep on a cloud.

I'm falling asleep on a cloud.

Trembling, Neena repeated it until she believed it. Until she fell asleep.

THE HISTORY OF American forestry was rooted in Pisgah. The Cradle of Forestry, located twenty miles south of Deep Fork, was the country's first forestry school, and it still existed to this day. Josie had gone there on a field trip in the third grade, where they had sifted through decaying leaf mold to search for creepy crawlies. Her favorite sneakers with the rainbow heart shoelaces had gotten muddy.

Josie hadn't felt cradled by the forest then, and she didn't feel cradled by it now as the first rays of light pierced through the canopy. She had managed two, maybe three, hours of restless sleep, hounded by stressful dreams and intrusive thoughts. She wasn't an early riser. On the rare day without school or work, she slept well into the afternoon, unlike Neena, whose parents always guilted her out of bed by eight o'clock.

Josie checked her phone, which was still attached to the charger. 5:51 a.m. How obscene.

Like a reflex, her fingers opened the weather app, forgetting that it wouldn't be able to connect to a cell tower. The blue light of her screen froze and then blackened—but not before she noticed the battery indicator.

"Shit," she said.

Neena stirred at the muttering. "What is it?" She sounded groggy but coherent. Her body was curled into a tight ball, and Josie suspected that she'd had even less sleep.

"My phone. It was at thirty-one percent, but it died. Just like that." Josie checked the charger's cord, but both ends were firmly attached. She pressed the charger's buttons. None of its lights came on. "The charger's dead, too."

"What?" An arm reached out from the confines of Neena's sleeping bag. It snatched up her phone. "Mine won't even turn on," she said a moment later.

"Shit. *Shit.*"

"They were fine last night."

Josie put on her glasses to inspect the situation more clearly. "Maybe the cold killed the batteries? I've heard that can happen."

"The charger's dead, too?"

"That's what I said."

"But . . . how is that possible?"

"I guess it also lost its charge in the cold. Or, I don't know. Maybe we forgot to charge it before we left."

"You *forgot* to charge the charger?"

"No! I remember doing it." Josie's thoughts swam. Yesterday morning had been a blur of preparations. "I'm just saying . . . I don't know. No. I'm sure it was the cold."

"So, what?" Neena lifted her head. "That's it?"

Josie threw up her hands. *Do you see a charged phone anywhere?*

"Oh my God. Just when I thought this trip couldn't get any worse."

Even though Josie felt the same way, it still smarted to hear Neena say it. "So, what do you want to do?"

"What do you mean? They're dead. There's nothing we *can* do."

"I meant, today. Do you want to keep hiking? Or do you want to go home?"

Neena sighed. Her fingers templed against her forehead. "I don't know."

Neither of them spoke. The silence was tense.

"Well," Josie said. "We still have a map. And the trail has been pretty obvious, so far."

"Except for this campsite."

"Yeah, but we'd be staying in an open area tonight. We could put the tent anywhere."

"Look at you, suddenly the optimist."

Josie reddened. "I'm just saying, if you want to keep going, we can keep going. We still have the printouts. The only things we've actually lost are our cameras. But if you want to head back—"

"Do *you* want to head back?"

"I don't know. I don't care! That's why I was asking you."

"Well, I don't care, either," Neena snapped.

And that was the moment Josie realized she'd been hoping to salvage the trip. She'd wanted *Neena* to salvage the trip. She'd wanted Neena to beg and fight for it, but Neena wasn't going to push Josie to do anything anymore.

At an impasse, the girls forced themselves from bed. The atmosphere was sulky and dismal. Smoke still smothered the air. Josie peeled back her socks to examine her feet in the low light. They were swollen and ripe with tender blisters that would have to be popped.

After locating a safety pin inside the first-aid kit, she cleaned it with a baby wipe. Her skin, too. Neena remained silent but observed the surgery with attentive eyes. Josie refused to be seen as weak. With a hiss and a wince, she stabbed the ball of her right foot. Clear fluid spurted onto her sleeping bag. Neena grunted in nonjudgmental disgust as Josie coaxed out the rest of the liquid, then jabbed the other sacs in quick succession. Gingerly, she cleaned and bandaged each wound. When she pretended that it didn't hurt, it hurt a little less.

Wishing she had room in her hiking shoes to wear both pairs of socks, Josie pulled only the thickest back on. She loosened the shoelaces and wriggled her feet inside the shoes. It would have to do. The temperature seemed to be above freezing, but barely. Maybe the low forties. If so, it was almost ten degrees lower than what had been forecast. Josie caught Neena eyeing the extra clothing layers that Josie had stripped off in the middle of the night, as well as Josie's backpack, which had been plumped for pillow usage. Josie shoved her hat back on for protection against the morning chill.

Neena turned away with a tiny shake of her head.

"What?" Josie said.

"Nothing." But Neena was shivering, and her lips were tinged violet.

It's not my fault you didn't listen when Win said it would be cold. On any other day, Josie would have felt bad for Neena. She would have apologized for being unaware that Neena was freezing and would have offered her the extra clothes.

Today, she would do neither.

Josie unzipped the tent and stepped outside into the early light. Though the fog had rolled along to other mountains, it had left behind a glistening sheen. High in the treetops, the elaborate weavings of the fall webworm moth sparkled in the dew. Down on the ground, the marshmallow remnants of her uneaten s'more had glommed onto the pine needles. An army of industrious ants teemed over the unsavory memory. She shuddered, grateful that insects were all it had attracted.

The girls plodded away to relieve themselves. When Josie

returned, she dug out the filtration system and gathered their water bottles.

Neena materialized a few minutes later. "Breakfast?"

Josie held up the equipment.

"Great." Neena slumped, dejected. "This'll be fun."

Josie headed for the spring, but, after a few seconds, Neena still wasn't following. She paused to find Neena staring at their campsite.

"It just feels weird to leave all our stuff," Neena said.

"Who's going to take it?"

The girls glanced up the slope. The yellow-gold tent appeared undisturbed from the previous night. The structure was soundless. Lifeless. It made Josie uneasy, although she couldn't pinpoint why. Neena was also staring at the campsite with an unsettled furrow in her brow. Eager to get the filtering over with, Josie limped on.

Eventually, Neena trudged along behind her.

They hiked the five minutes to the spring without a word, reacquainting themselves with every ache, chafe, and bruise that had worsened overnight. Their task required filling a liter-size bag and then squeezing the water through a small filtration device directly into their bottles. Josie unrolled the bag and began to collect water.

"So . . . we didn't decide. Are we staying or going home?" The "we" left a bitter flavor on Josie's tongue. An off note.

Neena shrugged.

"That's not an answer," Josie said, exasperated.

"Why is it up to *me* to make the decision?"

The accusations from their fight were still raw. Josie angled her face so that Neena wouldn't see the tears pricking her eyes. "Fine. I think we should keep hiking."

"Fine," Neena said. "We'll keep hiking."

"Fine," Josie said, embarrassed at her own childishness. Aware that she'd made the wrong choice for the wrong reason.

• • •

The spring was only a few inches deep, and it was taking forever for Josie to fill the bag. The trickle out of the PVC pipe had created a shallow pool. Or maybe it was a stream. It was impossible to tell where the water ended—or if it even did. Neena couldn't fathom why Win had recommended this for their water source. The only reasonable explanation was that the flow had diminished since the last time he'd seen it, which begged the question: What else had changed out here?

The air resonated with the monotonous din of mosquitos and stinging yellow insects. Her head buzzed, fatigued and headachy, on the same frequency. Already she regretted the decision to keep hiking. She'd only agreed because she didn't want to be the one who backed down. What were they doing out here, wasting time by pretending that their friendship was still functional? She should be packing boxes at home. Savoring this final week with her family. Drinking water from a tap.

Her gaze hadn't left the bag. "Oh my God," she said, thrusting a large leaf at Josie. "Use this to help scoop, or we'll be here all day."

Josie seemed hurt and taken aback, but Neena didn't care, because her idea worked. The bag filled faster, and they were able to filter their first liter. In a resentful and protracted silence, the girls swapped turns and then lugged the bottles back uphill to the campsite. When Josie inquired about the bear canister, Neena pointed in its direction. *Get it yourself.* She plopped into a camp chair, shook her inhaler, and puffed.

"Really?" Josie didn't even have to raise her voice. "*This* was your idea of far away?"

Neena swiveled, startled. Under the spell of night, it had seemed far away, yet the canister was nestled beneath a pine that was twenty feet away, at most. Shame washed over her. Holding in her medicinal breath, she struggled for an excuse but failed.

Josie shook her head with disgust, as if Neena weren't speaking because she was unwilling. Neena exhaled slowly. She sipped her water, swished out the inhaler taste, and spit. *Now* she was unwilling.

Though neither girl was a coffee drinker, the chilly morning campsite felt like the right time and place for a cup of instant. Unfortunately, they hadn't thought to bring any. Breakfast was a protein bar each. Tuesday was supposed to have been oatmeal day—the protein bars had been rationed for tomorrow—and the warm meal would have been nice. But Neena didn't want to remind Josie or ask for any favors. And she certainly didn't want to keep hiking. But if Josie could keep going, she sure as hell could, too.

Taking turns inside the tent, they bathed with more baby wipes and a shared stick of deodorant. Win had warned them that bringing it would be pointless—it added weight, and the scent wouldn't last long, anyway. Judging from yesterday's odors, he was right.

Neena's hips were bruised like rotting plums. Shivering and goose-bumped, she exchanged her T-shirt for the flattened pillow T-shirt. A sweater would have been a better option, preferably one of those thick Icelandic woolly ones. But at least this shirt was dry. Between the puddles and sweat and fog, Neena had been moist since their arrival. She zipped her hoodie back up and hoped the sun would dry it out.

Josie shed her hat and underlayers and changed shirts, too. Both girls wore the same jeans as yesterday, although Josie's weren't damp. Her skin was blotched and ruddy from a slight burn. They both applied sunscreen and gallons of bug spray.

Tent and chairs were returned to their waterproof sleeves. It was harder to pack without helping each other, harder to stuff the sleeves with everything unfurled back to its full size. But the girls each worked alone. Once again, the food was loaded into Neena's pack. Josie had promised to carry it today. Neena wondered if Josie had forgotten, or if she was deliberately choosing to keep Neena's pack heavier.

They were ready to leave sooner than expected. It had taken a lot longer to set up the camp than to take it down. Neena glanced upward through the pines. The yellow-gold tent was still without any signs of life, but it was early. And if the tent's owner had been the person in the fog, then they'd returned late. It made sense that they would still be sleeping.

And yet. There was *quiet*, and there was *empty*.

"Where are you going?" Josie asked.

Neena climbed the slope softly, not wanting to disturb the mysterious camper. As she drew closer, and the campsite seemed more and more unoccupied, her curious steps grew confident. Two chairs similar to their own sat neatly around a similar rock circle. The seats were dusted with pollen and leaves. The stones and ash were cold.

She turned toward the tent. A sickening, eerie feeling overtook her.

"Don't," a voice said behind her.

Neena jumped, despite knowing it was Josie. "I wasn't going to," Neena insisted. But Josie was right to warn her not to touch anything. An hour earlier, Neena had even been concerned about strangers pawing through her own unguarded possessions.

Josie's hands settled on her hips. "I guess they're still out backpacking."

Neena assumed this, too, despite the fact that the campsite felt abandoned. But perhaps every dwelling felt this way as soon as humans left it behind. Perhaps nature reclaimed its territory faster than she gave it credit for.

The frightened sensation dissipated . . . and yet, the memory of the footsteps bothered her. She could still hear them disturbing the underbrush. Heavily. Steadily. Maybe it had been a deer, after all—an imposing buck stacked with antlers. In the tenuous light of dawn, the grass at the edge of the pines looked as bright as spring. It seemed possible now that the grass was always greener on the other side of night.

The girls returned to their own belongings. In their absence, a few pine needles had fallen upon Neena's pack.

ONLY A SHORT hike beyond where they'd traveled the previous evening, the Wade Harte Trail was finally freed from its claustrophobic tunnel and opened to the sky. At last, the surrounding mountains revealed themselves, layered and endless in every direction. Low clouds lent the impression of a distant mountain lake. Water trickled down a craggy rock face. Josie marveled, once again, at how the Blue Ridge Mountains were *actually* blue.

Pale blue, dark blue, purple blue. Her father had taught her that these colors were created by isoprene exhaled from the breathing trees. How peculiar that the same spectrum that made her surroundings so thrilling and wondrous had also warped her mind into such a vast and sucking hole. Her outlook had been blue for a long time.

She already knew how the rest of this trip would go: They were stuck, and they were stubborn, so they would be polite. When Neena dropped her off at home, they would lie stiffly about having had a nice time. A handful of bland texts would be exchanged before Neena moved away, and another would be exchanged during the first month of school. And then they would never speak again. Josie had been through this before with Sarah, her best friend before Neena. Finality loomed. Their friendship was heaving its last breath.

The elevation remained steady, and the atmosphere strained, as the girls trekked southward along the stony ridgeline. They were in the Misty Rock Wilderness now. Neither of them fully understood what was meant by this particular definition of "wilderness," but it had something to do with a federally preserved area of land. The Misty Rock Wilderness was still inside the Pisgah National Forest.

It did feel different, though. The temperature rose along with the sun, but the exposed high ridges were cooler and windier than the humid woods below. The terrain was sparser. The shrubbery had grown dense, but the deciduous trees had thinned. Everything looked a little thirstier.

Josie's blisters pulsated, and her heels were as raw as ground beef. What if she was creating permanent damage? Would trekking poles have helped? How did those even work? They made people look as if they were trying to ski across dry land. Vaguely, she cast about the trail for a big stick like a wizard's staff. Or a crutch.

The gentle but persistent up-and-down felt like walking across the spine of a dinosaur. The girls traversed the glistering-white, quartz-crusted summit of Misty Rock Mountain without celebration. The intense exercise had tempered their emotions. Rests were fleeting, and silence kept them moving. Moving was better than talking.

After another brief dip, the elevation increased more significantly as the ridgeline trail headed toward its next peak. By the time they entered into the treeless balds, exhaustion forced the girls to take a real break. They perched atop a rocky outcrop and ate prepackaged trail mix with an unusually high percentage of M&M's. Rolling mountaintops extended beyond them in every direction. The Appalachians were one of the world's oldest mountain chains. Once soaring to majestically Himalayan heights, they had been gradually sinking for millions of years. In time, they would vanish completely.

"Good trail mix," Neena said.

"Yeah," Josie said.

"How are you doing on water?"

"Good." Josie checked her bottles. "I have about a liter and a half left."

"Me too."

"That's good."

Good, good, good. What an empty word.

The girls unshouldered their packs at Burnt Balsam Knob around eleven. They guessed. They couldn't check their phones. Despite their aches and pains, the long hike to the turnaround point had been far less grueling than the previous day's shorter, steeper hike. Six hundred feet of altitude had been gained since the campsite this morning, but it had been across a distance of about five miles. The gradual incline made a difference. They were making better time. Somehow, this only made Neena feel more despondent. This summit was the literal high point of their trip, and it felt anything but.

They ate turkey jerky on an expansive grassy bald with yet another sweeping view.

"Do you think there was a forest fire?" Neena asked, wishing Josie would make the effort to start one of these stilted conversations herself. The bees were loud, droning and swarming from wildflower to wildflower. With a wrong move, she might get stung.

"Hmm?"

"*Burnt* balsam."

"Oh. Maybe." Josie ripped into a hunk of leathery jerky. She chewed slowly. Swallowed. "Or maybe it's because that stand of trees looks kind of black." She pointed toward the dark swath of forest beneath them.

Supposedly, this was the most popular section of the Wade Harte because it was the trail's highest point, and because the knob connected to several shorter, busier trails. But nobody joined them. Neena would have killed for a noisy family with a spunky labradoodle sporting a bandana. Anything to disrupt the depressing silence.

Her heart panged for home. Her family wasn't loud, but at least they would talk to her. At least they didn't think she was a selfish idiot. All morning long, Neena had toggled between hurt and anger, her mind incessantly repeating the unrepeatable accusations that she and Josie had hurled at each other. Now she was too tired to launch a defense. Stretching her muscles, she searched for an area to relieve herself. Despite the vacant crest, the whole area felt exposed.

A brass gleam caught her eye.

"Hey," she called out. "Come see this."

Josie ambled over with a wary gait.

WADE CECIL HARTE

1894–1962

CAPITALIST AND CONSERVATIONIST

WHO DEEPLY LOVED THESE MOUNTAINS

The plaque was affixed to a stone. "The man of the hour," Neena said. "You don't see 'capitalist' and 'conservationist' in the same sentence very often, do you?"

Josie hmphed. "Not anymore."

"Well, if entitled white men don't kill us first, climate change will." Neena paused as the wind shifted. The sweet scent of the balsam firs below rose to greet them on the breeze. It smelled like something precious that was about to be lost forever. "Nature always exacts its revenge."

After packing up their lunch, the girls headed back the same way they came in. They were halfway done, and Neena's gut twinged. Because the trip was a failure? Or because she was afraid of what came after the trip?

"It's all downhill from here," Josie said.

Neena wanted to believe that she was talking about the trail.

"Do you still want to take a different loop back?" Josie asked, about an hour later. She was standing beside a scrawny, overgrown path that branched to the right off the main trail. "We have a few options. I think this is the one that Win said was his favorite."

The sun was high in the sky. A choir of cicadas rose and fell in waves. Their winged undulations vibrated and thrummed, infusing the expanse with unsettled energy. This was the first time that Josie had been in the lead, and she waited for Neena to catch up.

For their return, they could either continue retracing their steps on the Wade Harte, or they could take one of these lesser-known side trails, created by hikers who frequented the area. The trails weren't marked on traditional maps, but they did have blazes that could be followed. Next to this side trail, nailed into the gaunt trunk of a lone evergreen, was a triangle made out of three beer-bottle caps—one cap above two.

"Win said it drops down off the ridgeline and wanders beside a creek," Josie said. "It'll spit us out near Deep Fork. There might even be some places to camp down there." The girls hadn't decided yet where they were stopping for the night. The plan was to unload their gear wherever looked okay, whenever they were tired. It wasn't like the previous night; there were plenty of places to camp inside the Misty Rock Wilderness.

"If we hike down," Neena said, "we'll have to hike back up."

"Not like yesterday. It only goes down a little."

Neena gestured at the bottle caps. "That's a blaze?"

After explaining the concept, Win had quizzed them about blazes. The girls had done well, but they'd already forgotten everything. Anticipating this, he had printed out a chart so they wouldn't get lost trying to decipher them.

"Yeah," Josie said. "It might be fun to play follow-the-bottle-caps." When Neena didn't respond, heat rose up Josie's neck. "It would give us something to do, at least."

Neena gave a deflated shrug.

Forced to defend a suggestion she barely cared about, Josie turned so that Neena could unzip her pack. "The chart's in here."

Your brother found the trail, and your brother had the gear. And you lean on him like you lean on me.

Shame and foolishness reverberated inside Josie, but she held her body rigid while Neena sorted through their papers. It was the closest they'd stood all day—the position no longer natural, but invasive. The chart confirmed that the pointy-side-up triangle indicated the start of a trail.

"If it sucks, we'll turn back," Josie said to no one.

Neena clumped ahead, leaving Josie behind yet again.

At times, the bottle-cap trail was obvious. Other times, not so much. But the blazes were generally within sight of each other, and the girls didn't venture far until they were able to locate the next.

One bottle cap meant *continue straight*.

Two vertical bottle caps—the top one just to the left—meant *left turn*.

Two vertical bottle caps—the top one just to the right—meant *right turn*.

It did feel like a game, and Neena begrudgingly admitted to herself that the distraction of the hunt was welcome. Though the trail wasn't official—and the bottle caps, which definitely left a trace, weren't permitted in this designated wilderness area—she assumed the forest rangers looked the other way because, without the markers, it would be easy for hikers to get lost down here, off the ridgeline and off the beaten path.

The girls had been back inside the woods for about an hour. Hidden birdsong accompanied them from blaze to blaze. Leafy trees and mountain laurel and ruffled ferns encased them once more in green. Though their view had disappeared, they still had the sky. If only they had looked up, they would have noticed it was no longer clear.

The trail didn't follow beside a creek, like Josie's brother had described, but instead crisscrossed over numerous slivered tributaries. Wild blueberries flourished under the canopy in unripened clusters. The berries should have darkened and sweetened in July, but the changing climate meant they were still pale and sour. Surreptitiously, Neena tried to eat one. She spit it back out. It needed at least another week to ripen.

She touched the nail in the center of a blaze. *Continue straight.*

The nail was rusty, the bottle cap faded. They were all Cataloochee Light, a cheap regional brand with a distinctive logo—red with tiny white stars inside a blue X. Neena considered the type of person who proudly drank Confederate-flag beer, and perhaps her shudder was visible, because Josie gave the tree a second look. Josie's eyes bugged, but she wasn't looking at the bottle cap. She had zeroed in on the trunk. Claw marks gouged its rough bark. Tufts of black fur had snagged in the stubs of missing branches.

Neena tasted the blueberry, still sour on her tongue. She thought about hungry bears.

A thunderclap rolled and shook the mountains. The girls jolted as if struck by lightning. They had been so absorbed with their task that the graying light had escaped them. Though it was early afternoon, it looked like dusk. The sky was ominous with heavy clouds.

"What do we do?" Neena asked as they scurried to the next bottle cap.

"I don't know," Josie said, equally helpless.

The sky opened. The rain poured. They were drenched by the time they reached the next blazed tree, and the rain still pummeled them even underneath its boughs. The roar was loud and all-encompassing. Their hair was plastered against their cheeks. Neena squinted to keep the water out of her eyes, and Josie's sunglasses fogged. They hunched together, gloomy and immobile, as the minutes dragged by—the sky dark, the rain unabated.

"Fuck it." Neena had to shout to be heard. "We're already soaked. Wanna keep going?"

Josie rotated, shoving her wet pack into Neena's stomach. "Get my glasses first."

Neena grimaced. Reflexively, she pushed the bag away, and Josie tottered.

"Hey!" Josie said.

"I couldn't reach them." Neena's peevishness increased as she dug. Her entire arm disappeared. "Where the hell . . . Why'd you shove them all the way down here?"

With a glare, Josie whipped around and snatched them up. The lenses fogged instantly, but at least they weren't tinted. She stomped toward the next bottle cap.

"Hold on!" Neena stumbled behind her, arm still attached. "I have to zip you up."

Locating the blazes no longer felt like a game. Progress was slow and arduous. The bottle caps were harder to see in the storm, and they had to travel farther to find them. The distance between blazes seemed to be growing. Josie was limping again.

"Blisters?" Neena finally asked.

"Blisters and regret." Perhaps yesterday this might have been funny, but Josie was churlish as she wiped her glasses again. "Where the fuck is the fucking blaze?"

Neena pointed ahead toward a circular nodule. But when they reached it, it was only a knot of bark. The blaze was nowhere in sight.

"We should backtrack," Josie said. "I think we've gone too far."

Hoping their mistake would soon become obvious, they returned to the previous blaze before searching in another direction. This pattern continued for what felt like ten minutes . . . twenty . . . thirty. They still had no phones and no real sense of time. The rainfall was relentless. Their shoes stamped the muddy forest floor with zigzag treads.

"I still think it's the orange plastic ribbon," Neena said, referring to an earlier discovery on a nearby trunk.

"I told you that just means the tree needs to be cut down."

"Yeah, but who'd bother with that out here?"

"The rangers, if the tree is diseased and they don't want it to spread. What else could it mean?"

"I don't know. To keep going straight, I guess."

"We're not following a *ribbon*."

"Okay. Fine." Neena seethed. "What do you suggest?"

"Ten more minutes. If we don't find it, we turn around."

"Turn around?"

"Do you have a better idea?"

"Yeah, we follow the orange ribbon!"

"That's not a better idea!"

They were shouting again, but not because the downpour, finally weakening into a drizzle, made it difficult to hear. The cease-fire had ended. Neena clutched at the sides of her head. "We should have gone home," she said. "I wanted to go home."

"So this is my fault?"

"I didn't say that."

"Well," Josie spat, "I'd rather be home, too."

"Then why are we here?"

"Because you made me! You wouldn't shut up about it until I agreed to come."

"Because you've been miserable all summer! What are you gonna do when I'm gone? You have no other friends, no interests. You won't even drive. Just because your dad died in a freak accident doesn't mean that you will, too."

A cold wall slammed between them.

Josie turned away and started walking. Neena watched her recede for several seconds, furious that they were still dependent on each other. "Where are you going?"

"I'm going home," Josie said. She didn't stop.

"You're going the wrong way."

"We *can't* go your way. We have to turn back."

"You're the one who wanted to take this stupid detour! I'm not turning around now."

"We don't know where we're going."

"We've been down here for, what, two hours? That'd be so much backtracking."

Josie spun to face Neena. Her expression was dark and impenetrable.

"Let's just go a little farther and see what we find," Neena said.

"In what direction?"

Neena pointed at the biggest gap between the trees, a natural pathway that seemed like a logical place for the trail to continue. "That direction."

"Why?"

"Because it looks right."

Josie gritted her teeth. "We have *no reason*—"

The drizzle stopped. Neena stared down the line of her own finger.

"—to believe that *that's* the right way—"

Neena sidled forward to inspect a towering red spruce. The rain clouds cleared, and the sky brightened. The sunshine felt discordant with the way Josie was still berating her. She cut her off. "Josie!"

Josie bristled with outrage—but then slackened as her gaze landed upon the spruce. On its trunk, at eye level, were two indentations the size of bottle caps.

Neena examined the ground, expecting to find the missing bottle caps resting in the moss. "They must have fallen off."

"Fine," Josie said, though her voice was tight with resistance. Obeying the missing instructions, she veered course to the left. "But we're still going home. If you think I'm spending one more night with you out here—"

"Or . . ." Neena peered closer at the holes. "It almost looks as if they were pried—"

A crash of sticks and branches and debris exploded through the woods.

Josie screamed as she fell into the earth.

CRACK. JOSIE'S LEFT fibula snapped as her left tibia punctured through skin. The fracture was heard before it was felt. Josie's vision blurred as she thunked to a splashy halt. Her heartbeat flailed erratically, and her face flushed blazing hot.

Even here, her first emotion was humiliation.

Even now, her first thought was, *Of course it was me.*

"Josie! Oh my God. Josie!"

Stunned, Josie blinked at her left foot, which was mangled around a gnarled root. Something was wrong. *More* wrong. She squinted. A thick hunk of bone was bulging out from within. Her shoed foot hung limply from her ankle, held on by torn muscle and bloody flesh. Pain and terror rocketed through her. She screamed again.

"Josie!" Neena was shouting, sobbing from above. "Oh my God. Answer me. Answer me, please!"

Josie gasped. "Something's wrong with my foot."

"I know." Neena's tone changed abruptly. She sounded peculiar, gentle, shaky. "You're okay. It's gonna be okay."

Josie glanced at it again. Sour nausea rolled through her. She whimpered.

"You fell into a hole," Neena said.

"I didn't see it."

"I didn't, either. It must have been covered with debris. You slipped in the mud and then slid right in."

"My foot."

"I know. Can you move?"

Fear, dark and glassy, descended over Josie. Neena was asking her if she was paralyzed. Observing Josie's expression, Neena quickly adjusted the question. "No, I mean, can you move your right foot? Is it still okay?"

Unsure—petrified—Josie attempted to wiggle it. It wiggled. The girls exhaled their collectively held breaths. Josie moved one arm and then the other. Everything . . . everything else—*oh God, the left foot was barely attached*—seemed to be working.

"Can you get out of your pack?" Neena asked.

Josie was lying on her back at bottom of the hole. It appeared to be eight or nine feet deep and only a few inches wider than she was tall—maybe six feet. Roots jutted out from the earth like grabbing, snatching fingers. Her left leg was ensnared a couple feet above the rest of her body. Her pack was underneath her. With a grimacing twist, she slid out from the straps. Fiery pain bolted up her leg, spinal cord, brain. She gasped in shock. Her arms freed, and she fell back against the cushioning pack. Tears stung her eyes.

Neena's voice cracked. "That's good."

"It *hurts*."

"I know."

A sludgy pool of water stagnated beneath Josie's buttocks. She looked up and discovered that Neena was a remote blur. She panicked. "My glasses!"

"I think they fell off when you fell down."

Josie squirmed, patting around until she located them in the muddy slush underneath her pack. But when she put them on, the frames were bent and sat wildly askew. Her final shred of composure vanished. She began to wail.

"It's okay," Neena said. "You can wear your sunglasses."

"I can't reach them."

"You can. I know you can. Come on, Josie."

"I can't move. It hurts too much."

"It's okay. Those are only a little crooked, right?" Neena disappeared above her. "Shit. Shit, shit, shit!" She was yelling now. "Help!" Her vocal cords strained to their breaking point. "Help!"

The forest didn't respond. Trees dripped softly as rain shed from their boughs. The surrounding emptiness was total and immense.

Neena dropped onto her stomach on the squelching ground at the edge of the hole. She stretched an arm toward Josie. Testing. Already knowing she couldn't reach. "It's okay. We're going to get you out." She sniffled.

"You aren't allowed to cry," Josie said. Snot oozed down her chin as she tried to unbend her glasses. They resisted. "You're not the one stuck in a hole."

Neena laughed through a sob. She sniffled harder and swallowed her mucus. She didn't know what to do. Feet weren't supposed to *dangle.* "Can you reach me?"

Josie lifted an arm.

Their straining fingers were nearly three feet apart. But, even if they could have reached, Neena wasn't strong enough to haul her up. She didn't even know if moving Josie was the right thing to do. Unless they made a brace? Out of what? Frenzied and distraught, she considered anything in her pack that might be retooled before realizing there was still the basic problem of getting Josie out. Her brain scanned for information gleaned from movies and TV shows. "We need to bandage the wound to stop the bleeding—I think," she said. "Is there anything like that in your first-aid kit?"

Josie put her glasses back on. Her breathing was short. "Band-Aids."

"Anything bigger? More, uh, bandagey?"

Josie suddenly cried out, and Neena lunged back into her pack with an inspired recollection of T-shirts in action movies. Tomorrow's clean shirt proclaimed in bold type that she was a PAWNEE GODDESS. She ripped it. *Tried* to rip it. As she bit down, the fabric squeaked unpleasantly against her teeth. With more precision, she bit again and rubbed with her canines until a hole formed. "Aha!" It sounded maniacal—she felt maniacal—as she wriggled a finger inside the hole and ripped.

"Pads," Josie said.

Neena tore the shirt into a strip. "What?"

"Pads. In your bag."

"Oh my God. You're a genius." Four menstrual pads were left—clean, sanitary, and absorbent. Neena laid them out before attending to her patient. Her patient that she still couldn't reach. The ankle gaped open like the slit of a lewd mouth. A knob of bloody bone and pink muscle protruded from the skin. The dangling foot rocked in the air.

Neena's throat convulsed, and she retched, nearly vomiting. *Pull yourself together.* She had a vision of long white casts in hospital beds. Legs raised in spidery contraptions. "I need you to be brave, Josie. I need your help. You're the one who has to do this."

Josie's eyes spilled over with fresh tears. "No."

"Tap into that adrenaline, okay? We're gonna untangle your foot, and then we'll use that same root to elevate it." Neena prayed this was the right thing to do, but at least keeping it elevated would prevent more blood loss. Maybe? "One step at a time. First, I need you to scoot your butt forward so you can reach the root."

"I can't."

"You have to."

"I can't."

"On the count of three," Neena said harshly. "One. Two. *Three!*"

Josie scooted and screamed. Her vision spotted and fuzzed in electric bursts, fuses burning, as Neena handed down the supplies and barked the orders. The pain sizzled. Her ankle and foot became a singular *it*, separate from the rest of her body, as she complied with Neena's sadistic demands. She unsnagged it. Cradled it. Supported it with pads. *Support the gap, not too tightly. Wrap it, wrap it!* Wrapped the whole thing in cloth. Woozy with agony, Josie blacked out. Only for a second. She was screaming again.

Lie back, Neena was shouting.

Breathe, Josie. Deep breaths. You did so well.

Breathe with me.

Josie found her breath and clung onto it. Her pulse was going haywire. She goggled at her ankle, fatly wrapped in feminine hygiene products and bandaged with the T-shirt, her mind blank with trauma.

"Can you hear me?" Neena said. "I'm going to get help."

Josie's pupils widened in fright. "No."

"I can't get you out on my own. I'm sorry."

"You can't leave me. Please don't leave me."

Their eyes locked through Josie's lopsided glasses.

Neena's heart shattered into spiky fragments. "I'm leaving my stuff here so I can run faster. It'll still take a few hours, but at least it's mostly downhill. I'll plug my phone into my car's charger, drive until I get a signal, and then I'll call emergency services and bring them back with me. I'll only be gone for a few hours—I promise."

"It'll be dark."

"Only for a few hours. I'll be back so soon."

Josie's complexion blanched. "I don't want to be alone."

"I know, sweetie. It'll be okay." Hurriedly, Neena rummaged through her belongings. *Hoodie.* She put it on. *Headlamp.* She hung it around her neck. *Water.* She'd have to carry the bottle. What else? "Car keys," she said, stuffing them into a hoodie pocket. "What else? What else?"

"Phone?" Josie asked.

"Oh my God." It seemed unbelievable to Neena that she'd almost forgotten the one thing she never forgot. She snugged the phone into her back jeans pocket, where it felt safer because she'd be able to feel it the whole time. Paranoid, she moved the keys to her other back pocket.

"Food?"

"It'd weigh me down. You should have it." As Neena searched for the safest place in the hole to drop the hefty canister, the shiny metallic wrapping of a protein bar winked at her from behind the clear plastic. Changing her mind—*don't be stupid, you might need the energy*—Neena grabbed and pocketed it. Then she crawled onto her belly and lowered the canister so that it wouldn't have as far to fall.

The canister reached Josie without incident. She hugged it like a teddy bear for comfort. "Which way are you going?"

"The way we came in. Maybe it's faster the other way, but I'm afraid I might run into more missing blazes and get lost."

"Okay."

"Don't move your leg. And drink lots of water. You can reach it, right? I'll be back soon, so don't dehydrate yourself. And eat."

Josie lifted a trembling arm. "Be careful."

Neena reached toward the tips of Josie's grubby, outstretched fingers, hoping that she could reach them this time. She couldn't. Instead, she mimed squeezing them tightly. And then she was gone.

APART

JOSIE

THE LEAVES WERE still clinging, hopeful and green. They didn't realize that their time was almost up. That soon they would yellow and wither and brown, and fall to the forest floor. Their skeletons would grow brittle and crumble. Rubbery worms would swallow them up and shit them out. Their bodily remains would enrich the soil, feeding and fortifying new life, but their true forms would never be seen again. They would be ghosts.

With her glasses askew, Josie's world had split. Her depth perception was gone, and neither eye could see in perfect focus. The leaves above were an Impressionistic blur. The sky seemed weak and anemic, and the storm had left behind wisps of streaky clouds.

Among all of her meticulously rationalized disaster scenarios, she had never imagined breaking her bones and being left alone. Being left *behind*. But how fitting that it was her—not Neena—trapped in the middle of the woods. It would have been downright poetic if it weren't so goddamn typical. What kind of hapless loser fell into a hole? It was like a cartoon, if Bugs Bunny had ever been stupid enough to be tricked by one of Elmer Fudd's traps.

Too deep to have been dug by hand and too remote to have been dug by machine, Josie had concluded that it must be a sinkhole. It was roundish in shape, all earth and roots, apart from a skinny rhododendron that grew out from the side near the top. Branches poked underneath her body, too. They had probably been covering the hole and had come down with her in the fall. This was the most comforting narrative—that she hadn't noticed the hole because nature had hidden it. It wasn't her fault.

Sinkholes were common around here, but the only one she'd ever seen was in the parking lot of a vacant building on Merrimon Avenue last year. She and Neena had taken a special trip just to peer down into the newly ruptured asphalt. At the time, she had been unimpressed. The darkness had been vague and bottomless.

Josie cried softly. The pain was as lonely as it was agonizing. Hovering gnats whined around her face. When she waved them away, they pestered double. Her skin was pink and warm. A warm body temperature was good, though, right? At least her breathing had stabilized. And her blisters weren't bothering her anymore. Ha.

Having never broken a bone before, she hadn't expected it to be so revoltingly *auditory*. That snap. How many months had it taken for Win's arm to heal after he had attempted to slide over the hood of their dad's sedan like a cool detective in a B-movie? "Action cop," he'd called the move. He'd had that dumb bowl haircut back then, and her little-kid, chicken-scratch signature had taken up most of the space on his cast. He'd gotten so mad at her for that.

A few years later, her father's car was the scene of a second accident when a refrigerator slipped from the back of a pickup truck driving in front of him on I-240. The driver hadn't wanted to pay Best Buy to deliver it. Instead, he was charged with manslaughter for not securing it properly, and he went to prison.

He was out now. Josie's father was still dead.

The brute power of vehicles terrified her, but equally frightening was the idea that one careless slip could cost somebody their life. Josie began to collect stories about mistakes and tragic accidents. People who fell off cliffs while taking selfies. People who were killed by foul balls while watching baseball games. People who choked while eating competitively, were sucked into jet engines while repairing them, were impaled by fence posts while playing tag. People who fell into sinkholes while backpacking in the woods.

In the ninth grade—only a year after her father died—she'd had a panic attack during the behind-the-wheel training of her driver's ed course. The teacher had passed her anyway, out of pity, but Josie was still too afraid to apply for her limited learner's permit. She had leaned heavily on Neena's father to drive her around and then, later, on Neena. She felt safe with them. They were responsible. She didn't feel as safe with her mother or even Win, who drove too fast and didn't always signal. With Neena leaving, Win had been urging Josie all summer to get back behind the wheel, but he didn't realize that time hadn't lessened her fears. It had expanded them.

Proving her point that the world was dangerous, however, was not a satisfying victory.

How long would it take for Neena to return? And who would arrive with her? Josie imagined a team of medics sliding down the ropes of a helicopter, racing down the Wade Harte with a stretcher. The ring of uniformed adults would scrutinize her from above and scold her for being careless. How much did a rescue and evacuation cost? Her mom would be in debt for years to come. The gulf of shame widened.

Josie would have to start college in a wheelchair. At bare minimum, in one of those clunky Velcro-strapped boots. What if it took so long for help to arrive that her foot became infected? What if she lost it altogether thanks to sepsis or gangrene or any of those other conditions she'd heard about but couldn't actually define? She visualized coming to in a sterile room and groping down the side of her leg—only to discover the lower half was missing. The doctor would be harsh and ill-mannered. The nurses, stern but sympathetic. Her sobbing mother would cradle her, assuring Josie that she could still lead a full and fulfilling life.

It would be true, of course. It would also be devastating.

It's only a foot.

But it was *her* foot. How long would it take to learn how to walk again? Was a prosthesis hard and smooth like a mannequin, or did the plastic have some softness and give? Or were they all metal these days? Those good prosthetic blades, the ones athletes wore, had to be expensive. *Oscar Pistorius.* She'd nearly forgotten the man on the cover of the glossy magazines from her childhood. He was a Paralympic athlete, the first double-leg amputee to participate in the Olympics. He had been so cool, until he murdered his girlfriend. Then he was on even more magazines.

Josie continued to catastrophize. She began to think of her injured leg as already gone, a phantom limb, and it twitched in self-pitying outrage. Perhaps the rescue team would *never* find her, and she would starve to death like the deer they'd seen the previous afternoon. The same carrion birds would claw into her flesh and peck out her eyeballs.

Or maybe an internal injury, something unknown, would kill her first. How many people would attend her funeral? The turnout would be poor, she decided, which felt irresistibly worse. And Neena would be destroyed. This felt both terrible and gratifying.

The rainwater evaporated, but Josie's ass remained submerged in the dormant puddle. The afternoon sun baked the mud onto her skin. The light forced her eyes into a squint. Maybe she *could* reach her sunglasses. Delicately, her arm stretched behind her head, and she fumbled to unzip her pack. The top pouch opened tooth by tooth. As her fingertips groped, something small fell out. She shifted for a better angle, and pain shot through her. It ripped and blinded. She gasped and hissed. The pain was a chasm, and, as she strained to touch every item, she plummeted all the way down.

Best she could tell, the sunglasses weren't there. Maybe they had dropped out during the shuffle in the storm.

Her hand dropped and clenched, digging into the branches and mud. Josie screamed. Wept. Tore at the earth until, unexpectedly, she grasped the small object that had fallen from her pack. Recognizing it, she yanked it free and drew it to her lips.

The sound pierced the woods. Birds scattered from the treetops.

Josie squeezed the emergency whistle so tightly that the orange plastic bit into her fingers. She whistled without knowing or caring who she was trying to call.

NEENA

NEENA WAS HALFWAY back to the Wade Harte Trail before realizing that she'd forgotten her inhaler. The journey had been so much lighter without her pack. She'd run. She'd *flown*.

And then she'd jogged.

"Jogged" was a bullshit way of saying that she was running slowly because she didn't have the strength to run fully. Her adrenaline had vanished at the first indication of tightness prickling her chest, but that prickle was merely a caution. Not even a warning. She stopped before the coughing could begin, checked in with her lungs, and sipped her water. Her asthma wasn't mild, but she dutifully puffed her steroid inhaler every morning and night, so the medicine was already built up in her system. And she'd used the rescue inhaler—the fast-acting, emergency inhaler—this morning, too. She would be fine.

She would have felt *better* if she had remembered to grab the rescue inhaler, but there had been the foot. Josie's mangled foot. The foot had been distracting.

An estimated six or seven miles stretched between her and the car. Returning for the inhaler would mean an additional hour of jogging—the last thing she wanted—so Neena continued to retrace their prints through the mud. With her sharpened gaze, she felt like a hunter stalking its prey, except . . . by following her own tracks, didn't that mean she was *also* the prey?

The path grew difficult to make out once Neena reached the pre-storm tracks. The footfalls weren't as deeply imprinted, and many had washed away. Supplementing with the bottle caps, which took longer to find, her progress further slowed.

She would be fine. Josie would be fine.

They'd both be fine, and everything was fine.

The rainfall evaporated, but her clothing remained soaked with sweat. She yearned for dryness. *Fluffy bath towels and ionic hair dryers.* Would she have to run back with the emergency responders, or would they fly out in a helicopter? *Shea butter lotion and freshly laundered pajamas.* Did you have to actually be missing—or near dead—to get a helicopter? *A mattressed bed and cool summer linens.* What level of emergency was a teenage girl with a broken foot stuck inside of a hole?

But it wasn't just a broken foot. The graphic injury was most likely a compound ankle dislocation. Again and again, Neena rehearsed the plan in her mind: Get to the car and call 911. Then, call her parents. Then, Josie's mom. A mixture of premature anxiety and humiliation surged through Neena. Their parents would be frantic, but, even worse, they would be disappointed. She and Josie had failed their first test at being self-reliant adults.

As the bottle-cap trail left the forest floor and headed steeply upward to meet the ridgeline, Neena cursed herself and Josie for deciding to leave the main trail in the first place. She hadn't even reached it yet. The mileage technically hadn't even started.

An unknown noise pierced the forest chatter.

The fine hairs on her neck stood alert. Quiet rippled out as every woodland creature strained to place the sound. It seemed far in the distance, though she couldn't tell in which direction. But the noise was human-made, and it was insistent.

The answer crashed into her like an avalanche. *The whistle.*

Had Josie's condition worsened? Was she asking for Neena to return, or was she calling out for help from somebody else? Why hadn't they thought to teach themselves any whistle signals or codes?

Neena booked it toward Josie. Seconds later, she stomped back toward the ridgeline. The whistling stopped. She spun around again. A growl of frustration escaped, snowballing into a yell, and she screamed Josie's name.

Her heart floundered. The scream was futile. Josie wasn't close enough to hear it, and Neena wasn't close enough to turn around. But what if Josie's condition had worsened, and she needed immediate assistance? Or, what if another hiker had found her, and they were signaling for Neena to return? Then again, what if Neena did return, but then found Josie in the exact same condition? Or, what if her condition *had* worsened, but Neena still couldn't help? Either way, Neena would only be prolonging the agony.

Even though it felt deeply wrong to ignore Josie's cries for help, Neena chose to jog away.

JOSIE

WAS IT UNSAFE to fall asleep, or was that only for concussions? With a shot of disoriented panic, Josie touched her forehead, expecting blood.

Her head was fine.

She settled back against her pack. Everything hurt, though it was tolerable if she didn't move. The hole was muggy, and her eyelids were heavy. Mud caked on her skin in reptilian flakes. Hazily, she flicked off the scales. Here, there. Wherever the crust peeled up. Her body smelled of the warm woods—of dank verdure, crumbling soil, and rotting vegetation. How fitting if the sinkhole collapsed and the earth swallowed her whole.

After her father died, nature overtook their house. Yellow pollen floated in through the window screens and nestled into the cracks of the furniture. Dust thickened and transformed into grime. Greasy dishes crusted in tottering stacks, and abandoned saucepans molded with woolly spores. Rodents appeared, drawn by the glazy smears and scattered crumbs, and shit their droppings along the baseboards and into the open drawers. Photographs faded on the fridge and weren't replaced. Appliances broke and weren't fixed. Tree limbs fell and weren't hauled away. Weeds decimated the flower beds and annihilated the unmown lawn. Josie and Win taught themselves how to do laundry, but even their clean clothes were heaped in piles like discarded corpses.

When Josie became friends with Neena, she tried to block her from knowing or seeing, but Mr. and Dr. Chandrasekhar had insisted on meeting her mother. Shortly after, their house had magically opened to Josie after school. She was absorbed into their afternoon and evening routines. She did homework and ate meals at their table, watched TV and played Xbox on their sofa. The space was safe and sacred, and even after the counters in her own home were eventually scrubbed and sterilized, it remained her safe space.

Only yesterday, she'd wondered if nature might become her new haven. She had imagined spending months out here, trekking all two thousand miles of the Appalachian Trail from Georgia to Maine. Now, she'd either never leave or never return.

Had Neena reached the Wade Harte yet? Josie dreamed of it like a GPS map from above, following the moving dot along the ridgeline.

Go, she urged the dot. *Run, run.*

NEENA

NEENA BENT OVER in a coughing fit. Her chest was taut. The ridgeline was just ahead, but she couldn't continue to climb until her breathing had calmed. Steadying herself against a stalwart birch, she sipped more water. It was unrefreshingly warm and tasted like the woods. If only she had one of those ridiculous-looking pouches with the tube straws that people carried on their backs. Her arms were already sore from taking turns holding the bottle.

Spongy mushrooms with ribbed gills scaled the birch's trunk. Did the mushrooms harm the tree as they fed? It seemed sinister how fungus concealed itself—just out of sight—before erupting from the earth overnight, everything suddenly covered in mold and decay. Did it grow as quickly as it appeared? Or did it fester below the surface for weeks, months, even years before being pushed to its breaching point?

Josie was always future tripping; Neena had never known anybody more afraid of things going wrong. But maybe if they'd been friends before her father's accident, Josie would have been a different person. This idea made Neena uneasy, too. Would she have still fit into Josie's life if her father's absence hadn't carved out a void?

Somehow, the sinkhole felt to Neena like it was her fault. Like she had willed the danger into existence by denying its possibility. By not listening to Josie. Neena had said awful things, unforgivable things, but Josie had said true things. Neena *was* selfish.

When her parents had immigrated from Kolkata to Charlotte, her mother had to do her residency all over again. Her father had to pass the local bar. Later, when Neena was in elementary school, her mother had accepted a prestigious job at Mission Hospital, and they had moved to Asheville. Every day, her parents woke up at four a.m.—Ma to cook their meals, and Baba to commute the two hours back to his job in Charlotte. Ma would drive Neena and Darshan to school and then drive herself to work. Baba would drive home in time to pick them up from school. Yet they never complained. Neena had *never* heard them grouse about being too tired or stressed or busy.

They had sacrificed their own comfort to give their children access to greater opportunities. Every choice they made was for the people they loved, never for themselves. Darshan had followed in their mother's footsteps and was currently premed. Neena had rebelled and chosen a path that served herself. Not only was she turning her back on her parents' wishes, she was also abandoning her best friend—the one person who completely understood her and was always by her side.

Even now, leaving to get help . . . Neena was still leaving. Should she have tried harder to get Josie out of the hole? Her instinct had been to *go* and to *go fast*. It was the right decision, but it was also an uncomfortably close parallel to what was about to happen. Because even if Josie did find something or someone that she loved in college, she would still have to take care of her mother. By being healthy and successful, Neena's parents had given her the freedom to leave. Guilt chewed Neena up. She felt the dull, hot press of her phone in her pocket and wished she could text her ma.

Stop wasting time, Ma would text back. *This situation is not about you.*

Neena's selfishness burned everything it touched.

She pushed away from the birch and, a few minutes later, finally reached the Wade Harte. The daunting miles spread out, before her and behind her.

JOSIE

THE MOLD WAS spreading. Josie noticed it first in the bottom corner of a wall, an indistinct greenish-black spot, and scrubbed it away with a scouring pad. The wall dried, and the spot reemerged. As she scrubbed again, her eyes caught on another area, about the size of a quarter. She scrubbed this, too, before discovering even more. The spores grew fast, impossibly fast, like spilled ink or soured milk. She stumbled backward as they swallowed the wall and then shot off across the mopped floors and sterilized surfaces.

Chaos reclaimed her house in splatters of grimy, fungal watercolors. Josie glanced down at the yellow scouring pad in her hand, now blackened and rank, and discovered the darkness wriggling up onto her fingers. She dropped the pad, but the stain was already smothering her wrists, overtaking her arms. She ran to the sink, but the faucet was dry. She ran to the door, but the knob wouldn't turn. She ran to the windows, but the sashes were sealed shut. The mold crawled over her skin, alive and devouring—

Josie woke with a racing heart. An insect horde was swarming inside the sinkhole. Mosquitos, gnats, and flies vied for her immobilized body, attacking her exposed skin. Their host cried out. Flapping and waving her arms, she forced them off, but they careened straight back. Josie swatted them against her bitten flesh. She fumbled for the bug spray and bombed them. Her tormenters hurtled away.

Alone in the poisonous mist, she coughed and gagged. She leaned her head back to try and gulp at the fresh air, but it was too high to reach. Though the clouds had moved along, the wan color of the late-afternoon sky had barely changed. It was impossible to tell how long she'd been asleep. Her body spasmed. The buzzing wings haunted.

Slowly, then rapidly, her sunburn reintroduced itself. Her skin was angry pink and screaming hot, inflamed in the areas where she'd flicked off the dried mud. If only she'd remained covered in it like an adorable baby elephant. If only she'd remembered to reapply sunscreen at lunch. If only she hadn't fallen into this hole.

If only they'd never gone on this trip.

Her mind retraced the minutes before her fall. Getting lost, fighting. What were the chances of both bottle caps falling off the tree, anyway? What kind of rotten luck was that? Unless it hadn't been luck at all. She considered the rubbed-away bark on the other tree. The handwritten log of bear sightings scrawled across the plywood notice board at the trailhead.

She spun the stone ring around her finger in her usual nervous habit. It moved with resistance, tight from the heat. Less than a week after they'd bought the rings, she'd dropped hers into a cast-iron sink. It had shattered on impact. She'd had to borrow money from Win to replace it but had never told Neena, because she didn't want her to believe that this new ring meant anything less. Josie was careful with it now, always touching its smooth finish to ensure that it was safe.

She thought she'd been safe with Sarah. They'd been best friends since the first grade. But less than a year after Josie's father died,

Sarah had inexplicably abandoned her for a group of girls who had boyfriends and vaped scented clouds of cotton candy in the school bathrooms. Was it because Josie wasn't fun anymore? Because she worried too much? Because she was depressed? Maybe she put too much pressure on her friends to keep her happy. Maybe that's why they always left—the job was too big.

The bandaged mass on the other side of the hole was crusted red, but Josie's thoughts remained as detached from her ankle as it was from her. Her skin burned. Her bites itched. She fantasized about bathing, naked and clean, in a pool filled with clear aloe vera. The cold gel would hold her body aloft like gelatin. Protect her like a cocoon.

I could wait like that.

She placed herself inside the cocoon.

I can wait like this.

Something rustled in the woods. Her eyes popped back open.

"Neena?" Gently, she twisted, looking upward through her crooked frames. Her head throbbed with muzzy euphoria. She called out louder, "Neena?"

The rustling stopped.

No. It was impossible for Neena to have returned before dark. Unless she'd found help along the way?

"Neena? Is that you?"

Long seconds passed, and the noises resumed. As the shrubs shifted and resettled, her thoughts again sprang to bears. Her stomach plunged. The sounds grew close enough to become distinct— and then sharpened into footsteps. With unshakeable certainty, Josie knew the gait was human. And she knew Neena would have called back.

"Hello? Can you hear me?"

The footsteps continued toward her. Heavily, steadily.

"Help! Please help me." Her cries turned hysterical. "I'm in a hole! I'm down here!"

The footsteps stopped—just out of view. She was sobbing again, begging for a response. Something weighty and substantial was lowered onto the ground above her.

And then a man peered over the edge.

NEENA

THE JOGGING HAD ceased. Neena was speed-walking now, her formidable boots clomping low dust clouds along the balds. The hottest hours of the day were over, but the sun still persisted in the sky. She hoped to reach Deep Fork before dusk and to be down as much of Frazier Mountain as possible before nightfall.

Before this trip, Neena had never imagined that her upcoming separation with Josie would be anything more than locational. Their friendship was too strong. It could survive anything. Now, she wondered if she had been lying to herself the whole time.

She already knew she had been lying to Josie.

Freshman year, Neena's then best friend had joined the cross-country team. Physically unable to participate, when Neena had seen Grace running around the track with her new teammates—matching cardinal-red tank tops, ponytails bouncing behind them—she had felt targeted. Spurned. It felt like she'd been rejected for an entire girl gang. But the awful truth was that Grace had never rejected Neena.

Neena had rejected Grace.

Cutting the ties first became Neena's way of winning. Except the cold shoulder and ignored texts had only left Grace hurt and confused. Remorse had overwhelmed Neena, but, instead of apologizing, she averted her gaze. Instead of apologizing, she clung to cowardice.

Later, when Josie inferred that Grace had instigated the dumping, Neena had never corrected her. Partly because she felt sorry for Josie, but mostly because she still felt ashamed for how she had treated Grace.

It was shocking how quickly angry words—just like silence—could alter a shared history into insignificance. Neena knew Josie's order at Waffle House (patty melt with extra pickles, hash browns covered and capped). Where she kept her favorite lip gloss (Burt's Bees in Sunny Day, the back pocket inside her purse). How she couldn't roll her tongue (and rolled it using her fingers as a joke). Who her first crush was (Hiccup from *How to Train Your Dragon*). Neena was an encyclopedia of Josie knowledge, and now that book threatened to become as useless as the volume on Grace.

The surrounding panorama was lonely and foreboding. The sunlight was interrogational and oppressive. The clamor of insects shook the air like the tail end of a rattlesnake. Neena stumbled and gasped, overcome. It felt like someone was squeezing away her breath.

JOSIE

THE MAN WAS white. He wore a ball cap low over his eyes, and his body was broad and thickset. His beard was thick, too. He appeared to be somewhere in his thirties, maybe, and, though it was difficult for her to see his expression clearly, the energy behind his stare was intense. It sucked up all the air. He didn't speak.

Josie shrank, unnerved by his lack of reaction. Her sobbing ended in a wet hiccup.

"Well, I'll be," he finally said. "What're you doing down there?" His Appalachian accent was strong. It was the voice of the rural counties that surrounded Asheville, and the tone held a measure of accusation. Josie felt like she'd done something wrong as she tried to explain to him about the fall and subsequent injury.

His manner remained odd. Preoccupied. He was still standing, not crouching, as though he might take off at any second.

"I need help." She shouldn't have to state the obvious, except . . . it seemed that she did. Something wasn't connecting. "Can you get me out of here?"

The man glanced at the woods. "Where's your friend?"

Apprehension trickled through her veins. How did he know about Neena? How long had he been watching them? Was he the one Neena thought she heard in the fog last night?

He kicked at Neena's abandoned pack.

Oh. Though reluctant to admit she was alone, Josie couldn't see a way around it. "My friend left to get help," she said. *My friend knows where I am.*

"There ain't help for miles. How long has he—she?—been gone?"

It was only a one-word question, smuggled inside another question, but it turned Josie's stomach. Alarm bells clanged louder. She wanted to tell him that her friend was male and then later slip into the conversation that he was also a linebacker the size of a baby orca. But she was at this stranger's mercy. Facts were required.

"I'm not sure," she said. "A few hours. You didn't see her on the trail?"

"Which way'd she go?"

Josie hesitated—and then gave him Neena's location.

"She's your age? A teenager?"

Hesitated again. Confirmed.

"Naw," he said. "I ain't seen nobody. I came thataway."

Josie couldn't tell which direction he was pointing, and she didn't understand why he wasn't more concerned. If she had run into somebody in trouble, she'd be freaking out, trying to help. She would have at least asked the person if they were okay—even if it was clear that they weren't. But the man seemed calm and detached.

"Can you help me?" she asked again.

His demeanor changed so abruptly that she startled. With an interested step forward, he squatted to examine her. His eyes were dark and wide-set. His work boots poked over the rim. "You're in a mess, girl."

A whiff of sour breath struck her—an infected reek that hinted of diseased gums—but his countenance had lightened into a tease that expressed worry. Perhaps he'd only been in shock. Relieved at the change of character, she managed to choke out a laugh. For some reason, she was trying to make *him* comfortable.

"Can you move that?" he asked, referring to her foot.

"Not really."

"You shouldn't try."

"No," she agreed.

He shook his head. The gesture meant bad news.

Fear caught in her voice. "What is it?"

"Well, I sure hate to tell you this. I could probably get you out, but we might bungle that more on the way up. And if that gets worse—or if you lose more blood—there's a good chance you'd also lose that foot."

Faintness swallowed her. Distortion buzzed her frequencies.

"No," he said. "Best you don't move. Let them medics come to you."

"Do you have a phone?"

"Not one that works out here. Same as yours, I reckon."

"Ours died. Not that they had a signal."

The man thought for several seconds. He adjusted his ball cap. "How often do you girls come out here?"

"First time." She mumbled it because she was embarrassed. "Beginner's luck, right?"

"And your friend knows where she's going? She got a map?"

"Yeah, of course . . ." Josie cut herself off. "No. Shit. They're still in our bags. She knows where she's going, though. She's headed back the way we came in."

The man made an indeterminable noise. Turning away from her, he proceeded to rummage through Neena's pack.

"What are you doing?" Her heart battered against her rib cage. She felt protective over Neena's belongings. She didn't want this strange man touching them.

He held something up, and his concern grew more audible. "She okay without these?"

Josie squinted to make it out. It was the Ziploc with Neena's inhalers. The man's head cocked slightly—enough for her to understand he was processing the information that her bent frames had impaired her vision. Josie didn't want him to know that, either. The pain became vibrant and nauseating. She bit her lip, clenching to hold everything in.

"All right, now. Take a deep breath. You're turning purple."

"I think she's okay." The sinkhole whorled in dizzying spirals. "I'm not sure."

The man straightened. His stocky frame overshadowed her. "Right, then."

Her attention shot upward in distress. "You're leaving?"

"You ain't going nowhere, but your friend could get lost." His "get" sounded like "git." In one hand, he held the printout maps. In the other, he rattled the inhalers in their bag. "And she might need these."

"No!" Josie didn't like his company, but the thought of being alone again was harrowing. He needed to stay and protect her. In all likelihood, Neena was fine.

His dark eyes warned. "Don't try to move."

But if Neena *wasn't* fine, her situation could get dire. Which increased the direness of Josie's situation, as well.

"You'd only make it worse," he said, disappearing from view.

Josie's face pinched to avoid erupting in tears. She didn't want him to hear how upset she was to be left behind for a second time.

She heard him pick up the item that he had set down upon his arrival. From the bottom of the hole, she caught a glimpse—a flash—of the top of it. She couldn't be sure, but it looked like the barrel of a shotgun.

NEENA

NEENA WAS BEING hunted. For the last mile, she could swear that something had been tracking her from the forest below the ridgeline. A creeping awareness of movement had coupled with a visceral sensation of watchfulness. She tried to reason herself out of it. Being alone in the backcountry was unnerving, period, so her imagination was in overdrive. She was being irrational.

But then . . . a twig would snap. Or a branch would rustle.

And paranoia triumphed again over logic.

She reintroduced bursts of jogging back into her speed-walking. Her sporadic coughs were dry and hacking. Though she was well out of the balds, it was unclear how close she was to Deep Fork. She recognized enough landmarks to verify that she was on the correct trail, but not enough to gauge any real sense of time. The sooner she passed Deep Fork, the better. Her sweat chilled at the thought of navigating the dense tunnel of laurel in the dark with only the beam of her headlamp.

Shadows lengthened. Bees hushed. She raced the sun as it sank lower in the sky.

I'm sorry, Josie. I'm trying. I'm going as fast as I can.

A crack lacerated the silence. Neena shot out from her skin. Ahead in a nearby stand of trees, something had stepped on a stick. The foliage swished and splintered without wind. She hastened backward, pulse hammering, eyes scanning for beasts.

A man emerged from the cover.

He was an adult, maybe in his late twenties. He was white, lean and rawboned, with wispy patches of blond facial hair. His ball cap, rugged pants, and work boots didn't seem to belong to a hiking enthusiast, instead calling to mind the deer hunters who stocked up on Mossy Oak camouflage and discount Mountain Dew at Kmart. Though perhaps the gun enhanced this impression—visually jarring and slung so casually over his slim shoulders.

This was a different man. A second man. But Neena did not even know there was a first.

A certain pressure arose in her bladder. She glanced behind herself, suddenly terrified that she might be surrounded. She wasn't. She was alone with this man and his gun, and now that prospect seemed even more frightening.

"Shit, girl." The man drew a hand to his chest. "You nearly gave me a heart attack."

She was glad to hear that he'd been startled, too. And yet.

Yesterday, she had relaxed the instant the manly tenor was revealed to be the boy hiking with his girlfriend. The vibe here was different. Her muscles remained taut, her senses heightened. She didn't move to approach him.

"You must be the one I heard coughing," he said. "I was on the trail down there, but I couldn't see nothing. Thought I was going crazy."

His voice matched his appearance. It was the mountain accent that her future classmates in Los Angeles might think of unfavorably as hillbilly, or even basic Southern, but she recognized specifically as Appalachian. The South had a wide variety of dialects. Neena had met plenty of friendly and intelligent people with this particular drawl—those who dropped their gs and doubled their negatives—but she was ashamed to admit that she still felt nervous around the white people who had it. Or maybe it wasn't shame. Maybe it was something more practical.

Neena spoke cautiously. "Yeah. I kept hearing things, too."

Her gaze flickered back to the gun. Shotgun? Rifle? She only vaguely understood the difference, but its barrel was long, and it looked snug with its owner.

The man grew abashed and defensive. "It ain't for hunting. This rifle's strictly emergency use only. A few years ago, me and a buddy were chased by a mama bear protecting her cubs. We didn't get hurt or nothing, but I always come prepared." He adjusted the dingy shoulder strap and gave her a squirrelly grin. "Hey. Don't you go re-porting me to the rangers."

She didn't believe him—he'd brought up the subject himself and then denied it too readily—but it reassured her that he was probably stalking something illegal or out of season as opposed to lone female hikers. Still. It seemed best to agree with whatever he said.

"Your secret's safe with me," she said.

The man turned expectant. Like he was waiting for her to join him. Like he assumed they would hike together for a while and shoot the breeze.

Neena wanted him to either start hiking in the opposite direction or to hike so far ahead of her that she couldn't see him anymore—that he would no longer exist in her visible universe. Except, of course, if he went ahead of her, he could hide and wait and then lurch out at her from behind another copse of trees. And if he went behind her, she would never be able to stop looking over her shoulder.

She was trapped.

Reluctantly, she approached the stranger. A putrid stench reached her first. Her own body didn't smell like lilacs, but the odor emanating from the man was an assault. Angling her head aside to prevent gagging—hoping the gesture didn't look rude—her gaze snagged on the brush where he had exited onto the Wade Harte. The vegetation was thick and barely trampled. There didn't appear to be a path there at all.

"Listen, uh." She coughed again. "I'm kind of in a hurry."

His hands lifted in surrender. "Hand to Jesus, I won't slow you down."

Shit. *Shit.*

She began to walk at a brisk pace. "You said you were on a trail down there?"

"There's a bunch of them." He moved in step beside her, and she noticed a large hunting knife strapped to his belt. "I know my way around these parts better than anybody. Hell, I blaze my own trails."

His eyes glinted. They were small and close together, a washed-out shade of blue. His whole body was vibrating with a peculiar, jittery energy like he was tamping down some sort of excitement. Everything inside Neena shouted at her to run, but he hadn't actually threatened her or done anything wrong.

Also, there was the rifle. And the knife. She tried to stay a few feet ahead of him, but he kept closing the gap.

"By any chance," he said, "that wasn't you who blew that whistle a while back, was it? I called out and searched around, but I couldn't find anyone."

His casual tone rang false. Unless she was projecting it? Sweat beaded her armpits. She didn't want to tell him about Josie, but . . .

what if he could help? What if she was being racist against white guys with hick accents and ugly clothes? She hedged her response with a question. "You don't happen to have one of those satellite phones that works in the middle of nowhere, do you?" But then a deluge of coughing defied her attempt at nonchalance. She choked down some water but kept moving.

"Asthma?" he asked.

It almost stopped her in her tracks. Wheezing, she snuck a side-ways look at him as she wiped the dripping water from her chin.

His expression lit up. "I knew it. My wife—my ex-wife, we got married in high school—she had asthma, too. You should slow down, not speed up."

Neena didn't know what else to do but confess. "I didn't blow the whistle. It was my friend, who's hurt."

The man's footsteps faltered. "Your friend? What happened to her?" His eyes darted to the tree line. "Where is she?"

The feminine pronouns unsettled Neena. Was he assuming? Hoping? Yet the full, gruesome story tipped out of her in a torrent.

"Whoa, whoa, whoa. Your friend's foot's gonna fall off, and you're taking the long way back?"

Neena's lungs cinched another notch. "What do you mean?"

"You're headed for the parking lot on the other side of Frazier Mountain?"

She nodded.

"The Wade Harte ain't the *fastest* route. It's the *scenic* route."

"There's a faster route?"

"About a quarter mile ahead. Cuts straight down through the val-ley. I reckon you'd save an hour, at least."

Hope took a vast and fateful breath. "Could you show me where it is?"

"Hell," he said, "that's the way I was headed."

The man's pale eyes blinked too much when he spoke. His fetid stink curdled her stomach, and his gun was probably loaded. But perhaps he was a godsend, after all.

JOSIE

SHE COULDN'T STOP thinking about the gun. The man must be an illegal hunter, which explained why his initial approach had been so cautious—he didn't know who he was about to find. It also seemed possible that he'd hidden the shotgun because he thought it might scare her. Which made the gesture kind. Shivering in the dusk, Josie tried to convince herself that the man had only been trying to make her feel safe.

The trees above the sinkhole began to smudge like charcoal. The forest noises reshaped. Entire species of insects fell asleep as others awakened. The air didn't just feel colder. It smelled colder, too.

Josie put on her hat and draped her hoodie over her torso like a blanket. The puddle was still damp on her ass, and she couldn't contort her body into any angle that might allow her to reach her sleeping bag. She should have asked the man to toss down Neena's sleeping bag to her. He should have offered.

Her foot was still elevated on top of the roots. Her back and hips trembled with rippling aches that no amount of shifting could alleviate and that only disappeared whenever she accidentally jostled the horrific bundle at the end of her leg.

How long was it until nightfall?

She hadn't thought to give the man her name, nor ask for his. Why hadn't she armed him with more information? Her mother's phone number, at the very least. He'd reminded her, in a way, of her uncle Kevin, her father's older brother who still lived in Madison County, where they'd grown up.

Madison was only one county over, but the lines made a difference. Politics and attitudes changed. Income and education dropped. While her father had lost his childhood accent, her uncle had retained it. He was quiet and reserved and gave plenty of side-eye to the liberals in Asheville. But he was also big-hearted and dependable and the only relative who regularly visited her and Win.

He was a hunter, too. A few years ago, he'd taken her out onto his property and taught her gun safety and how to shoot. But, despite the lesson, Josie would never feel safe around guns. Because there was no arguing with a gun. When going up against one, the person without one always lost.

However, if Uncle Kevin—who owned a successful contracting business, as well as a small arsenal—were to ever discover somebody in distress, he would do everything in his power to help them. And he wouldn't be flashy about it. He would get the job done, and he wouldn't need thanks or praise. Maybe this man was the same.

She imagined her uncle's burly figure creaking in the rocking chair beside hers on his porch, teasing her about this "little mishap in the woods." Or her "little foot injury." Except it wouldn't be actual belittling. He'd be trying to make her laugh. And then her father would appear in the wrinkles around his sly, twinkling eyes, and he would live again for those few seconds.

The pain was unbearable. Time meandered and dwelled into oblivion. Hopefully Neena would reach the car soon.

Josie's appetite was weak, but keeping up her strength became motivation to eat. Tonight's scheduled dinner was chili macaroni with beef. A gift from Win, and she and Neena had been laughingly eager to try it. Not because the prepackaged backpacking food would taste *good*, but because it would be an *experience*.

Making the meal required boiling water. Josie poured tepid water into the pouch and waited as long as she could stand. In diminutive bites, she gagged and choked on the crunchy moistened shells and soggy compressed meat. She gave up quickly. Forcing down the last protein bar instead, she dreamed of hot mozzarella stretching away from a slice of pepperoni pizza. Sipping some water, she despaired for cold condensation slipping down a bottle of Mexican Coke.

These liquids reminded her of other necessities. With extreme difficulty, she maneuvered to urinate into the empty mason jar from the previous night's dinner. Some of it ran over her hands and slopped onto her jeans. *I should have just peed myself.* The thought wasn't funny. It was as honest as a deserved punishment.

A commercial airplane whined across the darkening sky. The sound magnified Josie's loneliness. She could see civilization, but it couldn't see her. She had no flares, no SOS spelled out in rocks. The passengers on board would never hear her cries for help. She watched the red blinking lights in silence.

The wind picked up with brusque and forceful gusts. Dead leaves swept across the ground and showered into the sinkhole. She gripped her hoodie tightly against her chest. *This*, she thought. *This* was the most sorry that she had ever felt for herself.

And then something unexpected blew into the hole.

It started with one piece of paper, then another. Then several more tumbled in behind. At first, Josie didn't understand because her mind didn't want to process what they meant—maps and directions and instructions, each sheet a memory from her mother's inkjet printer. The man had said he would bring them to help Neena. But he had left them behind.

Numbing dread sank over Josie. Her ears sharpened to the surrounding forest.

Night descended.

NEENA

THEY DESCENDED ON a narrow side trail off the Wade Harte. The man led the way. Neena didn't like how he kept glancing over his shoulder as if checking to make sure she was still behind him. As if her wheezing breath and crunching boots weren't enough reassurance. As if, at any instant, she might bolt.

The sun sank below the mountains. The final rays of daylight barely illuminated the trail. A nagging haze of gnats followed her. Visually and physically compromised, she swatted and stumbled down the slope with one hand clamped on the headlamp around her neck. It would be there when she needed it.

The man maintained a steady but incomprehensible monologue about digitally altered videos, trout fishing, his ex-wife, the judges on a network singing competition, pygmy salamanders, and phone addiction. She got lost in the connections and transitions.

Like the bottle-cap trail, eventually the path opened up, and the foot-worn rut vanished into the forest floor. Unlike the bottle-cap trail, the way to continue was unmarked. Neena's reliable internal compass—confirmed by the setting sun—was needling her northeasterly, so she was relieved when the man didn't break stride as he headed in the direction of the parking lot. It wasn't that she was worried he might get them lost. Clearly, he was familiar with the terrain. It was that she didn't trust him.

The man wasn't just a stranger. He was *strange*.

Something ferrety curbed his friendliness. His movements were scattered but quick, with purpose. It felt as if she were being shown one thing only to be distracted from another. Like that old man when she was in elementary school who waved her over to his car to ask if she'd seen his lost dachshund but then wasn't wearing any pants. She'd run away, hot with shame, feeling like *she'd* done something wrong. This felt like her fault, too. She never should have left the main trail. She began to pray to bump into another hiker, pray to reach the parking lot before dark.

They hustled deeper and deeper into the unknown woods. Somewhere nearby, water slipped and rushed over stones. The wind gusted up and shook the trees. And the whole time, the man never stopped talking. He swerved left around an ash with fibrous tumors of moss, and, expecting him to correct right and continue straight, Neena was surprised when he kept left—changing direction completely.

She hesitated.

Twenty seconds. That's how long she'd give him to start heading in the correct direction. Following behind him, she counted in her head. Upon reaching twenty, she decided she'd counted too fast and allotted for twenty more. Then it was only right to add another twenty because that rounded it to a full minute.

She wanted him to fix this. Now. Her panic spread like a virus. As one minute tipped into two, instinct overrode doubt. To prevent her from traveling a single step farther, her legs stiffened into a stop.

The man reacted like a trigger. His pale eyes bugged through the sooty black shadows. "What's the matter?"

"Why are we turning around?"

"We ain't."

"No." Something powerfully terrified detonated inside Neena. "We're headed back the way we came."

The man pointed behind her. "We came thataway."

"You know what I mean. We're walking back toward Burnt Balsam."

His pointing arm shifted. "Burnt Balsam is *that* way."

A blink of doubt. "No."

The story changed. "Well, hell. Yeah. But we have to go this way first. The trail's gonna loop back around." He took a few steps, attempting to shepherd her forward.

The problem was that no perceptible geological impediments existed that might require them to walk in this direction. This part of the woods looked exactly like the rest of the woods. Even the tumorous ash appeared to be random, as if he were following a blaze she couldn't see. She couldn't see much of anything anymore. Darkness had invaded the forest, and only one thing was clear: This man was not here to help her.

An unspoken transaction occurred between them.

The air congested with a toxic pall. In one swift motion, his mask of helpfulness vanished as the rifle slipped down from his shoulder and into his hands.

Perhaps he hadn't anticipated it—that she would anticipate him—because she had just enough time to bolt before the first shot exploded out. The boom quaked the earth.

Frantically, she zigzagged through the dark trees. Josie's voice screamed inside her skull as she tripped and bumbled: *Zigzag! Zigzag!* Branches slashed her face and snagged her hoodie. Brambles tore her jeans.

Another shot ripped through the woods. Bark exploded from the closest tree. The arboreal shrapnel stung her cheeks as the bang echoed against the mountains. *Zigzag! Zigzag!* Her airways narrowed acutely. The man tore through the bracken behind her.

She was choking, running, coughing, fleeing. She'd lost all sense of direction. Another shot, and she fell, but she'd only tripped over a root. Her wrists took the brunt of the impact, and as she swiveled to get back onto her feet, a slender gap revealed itself under the massive boulder beside her. A natural hollow. Flattening her body, she wriggled underneath. Too late, she realized that she'd entered the incorrect way, and her head was facing the wrong direction to see out. The squeeze crushed her breasts and lungs. She buried her mouth into her shoulder to muffle her coughs.

Inhale. She could hear Josie coaching her.

She used the muscles of her rib cage to breathe in.

Exhale, Josie said.

She couldn't exhale all the way. Every act was purposeful rather than automatic. Huge gulps of air felt like teensy puffs. Her eyes choked with tears as her neck tightened.

The man careened past the boulder—and then halted. No doubt, he'd realized he couldn't hear her anymore. How far away was he? A few yards? A few feet? She ceased trying to breathe. Her features twisted into a dimly rasping, openmouthed scream.

His footsteps trod back slowly through the undergrowth. Sinking into the ground beside her head, they stopped again. One way or another, she was about to die.

Please don't hear me.

Please don't look down.

Please don't hear me.

Please don't look down.

This was her final refrain. His boots shifted in the soft ferns, and she envisioned his stance following his eye line as it scanned the forest. Her abdomen quivered. She couldn't hold for much longer. The taste of ancient granitic bedrock, damp black loam, and milky green lichen infused her open mouth. Death had arrived at her tomb.

A bird made a startled caw as it flew from bushy cover.

The man shot again, and her coughing erupted as he thrust mistakenly toward whatever creature had frightened the bird instead of the creature hiding beneath the rock.

JOSIE

THE HOLE WAS black and clammy. Josie imagined the plastic bag of inhalers discarded in the fermenting leaves above. The printouts lay beside her in the mud. Night seeped in through the threads of her clothing and her sanity.

It had been dark for at least an hour, which meant that, any minute now, Neena should be reaching the car. If she'd made good time, perhaps she'd already done it. Help might already be on its way. Though it was unlike Josie to latch onto optimism, she placed a protective cage around these last glowing embers. Her ears strained for the distant notes of a helicopter or a team of emergency responders crashing through the forest. Sometimes she did hear them, only for the sound to persist unchanged and for her to realize that she was hallucinating in her exhausted delirium.

She heard four gunshots. They sounded like thunder. Perhaps they *were* thunder. But surely these were all delusions, too. The best-case scenario was that the man was only concerned with himself— and whatever animal he was hunting—and that he'd flat-out left the woods. Because if he *was* looking for Neena, what would he do to her? And if Neena couldn't get help, what would become of Josie? Would the man return for her, or would he leave her here to starve and rot? Which was worse?

Josie shivered. Her ears were cold shells, and her nostrils had hardened with the rusty scent of her own blood. The pain was so livid and fluctuating that it was almost redundant. Her only comfort was her backpack, the bulky presence hugging her from behind, the sole barrier between her and the surrounding dirt.

Night spiraled around her in lonely loops.

Two girls walk into the woods, she thought. But the story wasn't a fairy tale. They hadn't dropped a trail of bread crumbs, discovered a gingerbread cottage with sugar-paned windows, or shoved an old witch into a flaming stove. Nor was it a ghost story, traded in whispers around smoky campfires. It wasn't even an urban legend. Their story was flesh and bone. Urgent and real.

A firm crunch fractured the cloistered silence. The sound of an approaching human was definitive in its reality. "Neena?" Josie's voice surfaced as a croak. "Neena. Neena!" Each call grew louder and more unhinged. "Can you hear me?"

Neena would have called back. A medic would have responded, too.

"Help! Please help me!"

Heavily, steadily, the footsteps advanced.

"Oh God." Josie whimpered. "Please, no."

The steps were deliberate and unhurried. The man had returned, and intuition told her that he hadn't brought help. He stopped beside the sinkhole. Squinting upward through the inky nothingness, she tried to make out his figure, but he held himself just far enough back that she couldn't see him. Could he see her?

"Is that you?" she asked. "Are you the man who helped me earlier? I didn't catch your name. I'm Josie."

The man exhaled in the darkness. The sound was hushed, channeled through a robust and sturdy chest.

"Did you find my friend? Did you call for help?"

Each question swung ominously unanswered. Her denial took its final push in the form of honesty. "I wish you'd say something. You're scaring me." She managed a rough laugh to keep it conversational. "Is my friend okay?"

The man walked away.

But then he turned again, walked toward her—and kept going. As he passed the sinkhole, his large, shadowy frame materialized briefly before slipping back into black.

Fear stunned Josie like a captive animal.

The man retreated. Turned. Advanced. He was pacing, prowling, threatening her with glimpses of his presence. The hole grew deeper and darker. Hostility strangled the oxygen from the air. Intense anger radiated out from him, as well as something even more dangerous but stifled. A tangible manifestation of evil.

"Please," she begged. "Please stop. Say something."

He lapped back and forth.

With each predatory pass, her terror amplified. The man was enjoying himself. He was reveling in her fear. As his pacing drew closer, the outline of his shotgun became as clear as moonlight. Wishing for a weapon, she gripped the mason jar instead. Fright ignited into fury. "What do you want from me? Go away! Get the fuck away from me!"

In a flash, he was crouched beside the rim. She shrank back. The man stared, dark eyes unblinking, across the vulnerable length of her body.

She strained to see him better, to see him at all. "Wh-where's my friend?"

His shadow hardened. "No need to concern yourself about her."

A leaden weight dropped through her gut. "What did you do? Where is she?"

"I didn't do nothing."

Josie cried in soundless anguish. "Where is she?"

"I have plans for you."

"No. Please."

"I bet you love to party with the boys at school." His words vibrated with tightly bridled rage.

She cringed and recoiled. "Please," she said again. "Please leave. I won't tell anybody I saw you hunting. I won't say anything, I promise."

"Now, what makes you think I'm hunting, all the way out here?" The man paused to lift the gun. "This?" He laughed, but the utterance was low and malicious. "Yeah. I reckon you could say I'm hunting."

"Neena's getting help."

"Neena." His crude tongue tasted the name. "No. She can't help you."

An image appeared of her best friend crumpled on the forest floor, a vicious shot to the head, her gaze vacant. "Our parents know where we are. They're expecting us tonight. When we don't show up, they'll send help."

"They won't know you girls is gone for a while."

"They will. They're *really* strict. If we're late—even five minutes—they'll call the cops. My dad called them last year when—"

"Shut the fuck up," he snapped, dropping low to the ground. "I can smell a liar."

His halitosis stench blasted her olfactory organs, so abhorrent and animalistic that she believed him. Abruptly, he stood back up and stormed into the woods.

The crashing in the underbrush stopped with similar curtness.

Her heartbeat drummed. Seconds drained into minutes. She

concentrated for any noise that might betray his location, but the void had consumed him.

Her bones chattered and shook, and the jar of urine slipped from her grasp. She reached for it blindly before remembering the head-lamp. Her pulse leapt. As she shifted to reach into her pack, the frag-ile skin around her ankle—barely holding on to her foot—jounced with shockwaves of pain. One hand clenched into her jeans for strength, while the other patted through the pack's top pouch. Her fingers snatched up the headlamp.

She listened, vigilant, holding the headlamp dark against her chest, not wanting to waste the battery until the light was needed. The elastic strap snugged around her fingers. The plastic indented her palms. The woods retained their secrets.

If the man was gone, did that mean Neena was alive? Did he leave to check on her? Torture her? Was he playing sick games with her, too?

I'm sorry I told him you were out there. Josie clutched the head-lamp even tighter, hoping that Neena could read her mind, hoping the connection between them was real. *I didn't mean to give him your name. It just slipped out. I'm sorry that I didn't listen to you, that I yelled and called you selfish. You've never been selfish. I'm sorry. I'm so sorry.* Time crawled until she was positive the man was gone.

He wasn't gone. At first, it was a sensation. A prickle, a tingle, a feeling that something had changed. Her heart rate, having finally slowed, began to accelerate. Her ears perked but did not detect. But then . . . an inhalation.

Ice crystallized down her spine.

Exhale.

He was close. It didn't make sense that she hadn't heard his ap-proach, unless he'd never walked away at all. Unless he'd been stand-ing right above her the entire time.

Inhale.

Exhale.

Inhale. Exhale.

Each breath grew incrementally faster.

Inhale, exhale, inhale, exhale.

Josie struggled to operate her shaking fingers. They felt separate from the rest of her, a tool she'd never mastered. She pressed the headlamp's button, and the monster grunted away from the bleaching spotlight. It took a moment to process what was in his hand, pink and fat and wormlike. Repulsion quickly replaced confusion.

She seized the mason jar and hurled it. Glass shattered against the side of his head. His dripping face glinted, slick with blood and urine. He was stunned. And then he unraveled with fury. In swift retaliation, he picked up his shotgun and aimed. Her hand raised in defense as he fired into the hole. The explosion was the loudest sound she had ever heard. Debris and fluids blasted into a mass around her.

The man stormed into the trees. "Now try and get out," he called back.

She sputtered and choked in the aftermath. Her body was in shock. Warm liquid gushed down her arm. Her left hand fumbled for the headlamp and held it up. Floating specks of dirt glistered in the beam as she squinted through the settling cloud. She saw her right arm, which was still lifted in defense. But she did not see her right hand.

NEENA

AS HER HAND grazed the rock above, her ring scraped but did not crack. It wasn't the original. Neena had purchased it for a second time last spring, after the first had shattered when she'd banged it against her bathroom countertop at the wrong angle. She had replaced it straightaway with money from her savings, previously reserved for college textbooks, but she had never told Josie. Neena didn't want her to worry that the broken lapis lazuli was an omen—that it represented anything other than Neena's own carelessness.

The tight hollow under the rock was claustrophobically, suffocatingly black. It smelled of cold minerals and damp soil. Beetles and ants and grubs scuttled over her body, investigating the trespasser. Other invertebrates lay crushed beneath her, the same way that this stone—boulder, outcrop, whatever—was crushing her. Her rib-cage muscles hurt from having to force the act of breathing. Air was trapped in her lungs, unable to escape. She puffed out the old breaths. Gulped in the new. Through her pinpricked airways, it was like trying to suck up the oxygen through a plastic coffee stirrer.

After shooting at nothing, the man had erupted into an enraged frenzy. Bellowing and smashing through the vegetation, he would have been even more furious had he known that this outburst had concealed her coughing.

She had been hiding for a long time. The fear was endless and grinding. The man had been combing the area with greater stealth, in and out, on and off. She hadn't heard him in a while.

She needed to move.

She was terrified to move.

Was he still here or had he abandoned his search to look for Josie, instead? The idea was unendurable. If he found Josie, it would be Neena's fault. *I'm sorry, Josie. I didn't mean to tell him about you. I didn't want to. I don't know how he got it out of me.* Inside her mind, she saw her fingers unable to reach Josie's outstretched hand. *I'm sorry for everything I said, I didn't mean any of it. If you can just hold on . . .*

Dawn was still a long way away. Their families wouldn't recognize that anything was amiss until the afternoon, when the girls didn't come home, but they probably wouldn't start panicking until the evening. Help wouldn't arrive until nightfall at the earliest. She was the only one who could save them. Summoning a nugget of courage that she did not actually feel, Neena wriggled out from under the rock.

The cool whoosh of air was exhilarating. Unbound, she rolled onto her back, puffing and gulping in the wide-open night. She let herself breathe, exposed on the ground like an injured rabbit. Cloud cover had eliminated the starlight, but the dimmed quarter moon slowly began to illuminate the dark shapes of the forest.

It's not safe here, Josie said. *You need to move.*

Neena hoisted herself onto her trembling legs and took a tentative step. The noise was so loud that she froze. Where was she? Her internal compass was screwed, the compass app was on her dead phone, and the actual compass was still inside Josie's backpack.

A sound that had always been present separated itself from the din. Water warbled and flowed like indistinct white noise. It could be in any direction—all directions—but if she could locate the creek and follow beside it, the sound of the water might cover her movements. It might even cross paths with a trail.

The plan was terrible, but it was the only one she had.

Fearing the headlamp would alert the man to her location, she shuffled through the tactile darkness one leg at a time, tapping each like a cane. The ground was soft with rotting leaves and slippery roots. Perhaps she might trip over a rock, tumble down a ridge. Fall into a sinkhole. Her sodden clothes were freezing. Double- and triple-checking that her pockets still contained her car keys and phone, she rediscovered the protein bar and devoured it. The stale peanut-butter flavor parched her mouth, but her water bottle was gone, dropped somewhere in the fray. She crammed the wrapper back into her pocket. Seconds later, she changed her mind. After licking the silver lining, she dropped it to the forest floor. Maybe someday the litter might need to be tested for her DNA.

The man could be anywhere. He was in every hushed crunch, every splintered crack.

She listened for the coursing water in incremental tests. *Cold.* The rush softened. *Colder.* Darshan's giggly, high-pitched voice whispered to her from the trees, guiding her in a game they played when they were children. *Warm. Warmer. Hot. Hot! Burning hot. Fire hot. Lava hot. It's melting your feet, Neena! Don't you see it?*

The creek glistened before her with reflected moonlight. But it also contained its own source of mysterious light, slippery and quicksilver. The air shivered with the scent of undulating water particles. The sound was like a faucet filling a claw-foot tub, water agitating water, splashing and plopping.

Walking along the bank turned out to be impossible. The uneven terrain was too hazardous. A bullfrog croaked in a rumbling baritone, and Neena heeded its warning and retreated to slightly higher ground.

She followed the water downstream, traveling in the same snaking direction, hoping the flow would strengthen and lead someplace where she was more likely to encounter civilization. Of course, the flow might lead her *away* from civilization. Or over the ledge of a waterfall. But her parents' advice for lost children—stay put until somebody finds you—didn't apply tonight. The wrong somebody was already looking for her. She had to find somebody else.

A few feet away, something disturbed the brush.

She flinched and ducked. Her hands locked over her mouth. The noise was a low, whispered scurry. Were there mice in these woods? Voles? Moles? The stirrings were rodenty. She straightened, wobbly with respite. Arms extended and hands grasping, she fumbled deeper into the unknown. The shadows of the shadows tracked behind her.

On the Wade Harte, she had pushed aside her instincts about following the man off trail, believing that she was being paranoid, believing that he hadn't done anything wrong. But he had. He had made her *uncomfortable*. That was enough. She didn't have to apologize or make excuses. She didn't owe him—or any man, or any person—anything. She'd sensed what he was immediately but invalidated her own intuition.

Tears welled, salty, hot, and enraged. She felt ashamed for being gullible. She thought she had known better. It wasn't as if he was the first ill-intentioned creep that she'd ever met. Girls ran into men like this everywhere.

Her progress was slow and plagued with cowering doubt. Every step felt wrong. She was still stumbling and shivering when the eerie glow appeared through the trees. In English folklore, it was called the will-o'-the-wisp, but in North Carolina it was foxfire. Sometimes it was caused by the combustion of natural gases, but here it was from the bioluminescence of fungi and insects. She had never seen it before, only read about it. The mesmerizing pull of atmospheric light drew her in. Leaving the safety of the stream, she headed into the trees, but it was like chasing a ghost. The phosphorescent shapes kept changing and disappearing. Frustrated, she was about to turn around—the gurgling water was only barely audible anymore—when the lights reshaped again.

It wasn't foxfire. It was a campfire.

Neena saw it clearly now, so clearly that she wondered why she hadn't sooner. Dread warred with hope. Did the campsite belong to the man or to somebody else? Without knowing, she couldn't risk calling out for help. She was almost positive that she was still in the Misty Rock Wilderness, where fires were illegal. But sometimes even good people broke rules when nobody was looking. Right?

She slinked closer, conscious of every faintly booted crunch against topsoil as she moved from the cover of tree to tree. Stinging vines with three leaves brushed against her outstretched fingers. Coarse bark grated the tender pads. Heady woodsmoke reached her nose first, and then something else, something burnt.

The flames were lethargic and low. A shelter appeared through the wavering light. Constructed out of tree trunks and interwoven branches, the shelter was rectangular, almost tall enough for an adult to stand up in, and open on the side that faced the fire. Dark bulges inside gave the impression of camping equipment and gear. It was impossible to tell if any of those shapes were people, but the structure was large enough to hold two or three.

Nobody was tending to the dying fire.

If the campsite belonged to the man, it meant he had returned here after shooting at her. Otherwise, the fire would be dead by now. Nervously, furtively, she stole to the campsite's edge. Searching for life, she discovered none.

The scene was confounding. Something felt off, and it wasn't merely the absence of people. Perhaps it was the amount of work that had gone into the brush shelter; its permanent impermanence suggested that the same person frequented this remote site. Her confidence grew that the campsite was empty, but it wasn't comforting. Why would the camper—campers?—leave in the middle of the night? The only good reason she could think of was to go to the bathroom. Thinking of a bad reason was much easier.

The gear was mounded tantalizingly inside the shelter's cavernous black opening, perhaps containing a working phone or GPS device. But Neena remained still. The trees provided safety, and the moment she stepped into the clearing, she would be visible.

The campfire crackled. The insects chirred. Her surroundings gave nothing away.

She crept into the light.

The eyes of the woods turned upon her, boring into her from all directions. She broke into a scutter and ducked beside the fire. An unexpected warmth teased her body, a reminder that flames bestowed more than light. She crouched in to absorb their remaining heat, and her teeth began to chatter.

From this angle, two stumps or upright logs were suddenly perceptible. They weren't rooted into the earth but had been rolled here and positioned beside the fire like chairs. *Two chairs.* Hope flickered. A sauce pot rested on the ground near her feet. Hardened lumps in the bottom seemed to be a mixture of charred meat and baked beans, as well as the source of the lingering burnt smell. An eating utensil lay abandoned inside the pot, and a grill was still suspended over the fire. The cook had been either distracted or in a hurry. She poked at the dark lumps with a finger. The beans were cold.

A crack detonated across the clearing.

Her arms flew protectively over her head, but it was only the popping fire. Her hands lowered to clutch at her thudding chest—and that's when she saw it.

It lay on the ground in front of the trees, to the right of the structure and fifteen feet or so back from the fire.

It was a *still* thing. A terrible thing.

Her body straightened. Her heart thundered in her ears. She didn't want to go near it—she desperately wanted to run away from it—but this time, purpose overrode instinct. Forcing one shaking step and then another, Neena sidled toward it.

The whorling night kept it shrouded. *Run! Run!* She took off the headlamp from around her neck. *Breathe. Breathe.* Holding it like a flashlight, she clicked the button on. Its beam revealed the expected form, but that didn't make it any less shocking. The headlamp fumbled from her hands, hitting the ground and illuminating the bare purpled feet in appalling white light.

Both feet were still attached.

The body wasn't Josie. But it was definitely dead.

JOSIE

JOSIE'S HEADLAMP REVEALED a jarring dagger of bone and sagging strips of flesh. Everything past the wrist was gone. *Smithereens*, she thought. The man had blown her right hand to smithereens. She collapsed—but caught herself, mid-faint. Jerked upward with a stab of disoriented alertness. A fine mist of bloody bones, fingernails, and tendons had been sprayed across her body. She trembled and convulsed. Something hard tumbled inside her mouth. Without inspecting or touching it, she spit it out.

Her mind tweaked with shock. Inexplicable seconds passed in slow motion before the truth registered and a searing, transcendent pain shot up her arm. Josie cried out in astonished agony. How could something like this happen twice in one day? What were the odds? It was as if she'd been so deeply asleep that the first tragedy hadn't been enough to wake her, and the universe had been forced to double down.

Now, at last, she understood. Years ago, when she had fallen, the world had kept rotating without her. She hadn't known that it was her responsibility to get back up. No one could do it for her. But this pain screamed that she wasn't dead yet. This was her last chance. Did she want to live or did she want to die?

Josie wanted to live.

A determined focus washed over her. Vaguely, she was aware that the man had stomped away, but she didn't know if he had left or if he was hiding like the last time.

It doesn't matter.

If she were religious, she would say the voice was God or Jesus or a guardian angel. But this voice sounded like her father and Neena and Win and Uncle Kevin and her mother. It was everyone who loved her. It was the clear, convincing, empowering voice of survival. *Stay present*, it urged. *Take care of yourself first.*

She needed to tie off her stump—now. The hoodie was still blanketed over her torso. Locating the hole where the left sleeve met the left shoulder, she brought it to her teeth and ripped. The hole, once an embarrassment, was a lifesaver. The cumbersome fabric tore easily along the shoulder seam, giving little resistance until she reached the fabric overlap where it was sewn together. Her incisors gnashed, tugged, yanked. The sleeve ripped away. She laid it across her legs and centered the stump on top. When her skin touched the fabric, she bellowed. Every nerve ending was an excruciating live wire. With her left, nondominant hand, she wrapped the fabric quickly and tightly and then used her teeth to help knot it.

She fell back against her pack, gasping and panting. In shocked disbelief, she blinked at her bandaged arm. Her bandaged foot. Panic resurged, and she chugged half the remaining water supply before turning aghast at her blunder.

The voice returned to quell the cycle of hysteria. *Breathe.*

"Okay," she said. Anxiety would only jeopardize her condition.

Put on the hoodie. You need to stay warm.

"Okay." It was the only word she had left because she had to believe that everything *was* okay. She had to remain clearheaded. The left side was easy enough—her good hand, the missing sleeve—but the right side was a challenge. Her left hand held open the armhole and guided her right side through it. She bit her cheeks. Huffed to keep breathing. *Keep going. You're almost there.* Her right arm shoved through the hole, and the sleeve covered most of the injured bundle. *Zip it up.* Another difficult one-handed task, but it was comforting to have guidance.

Josie didn't speak out loud anymore. *Now what?*

Shh, it replied.

Wind chilled the woods. Her hearing strained through the turbulent tumble of foliage. She shivered in a cold sweat and cradled her right arm. Her right elbow remained cocked to keep the injury raised. Now she had *two* raised injuries. Blood was sopping through both layers of hoodie fabric. Hopefully, her grogginess was only due to exhaustion and stress. How much blood had she lost today? How much more could she lose? The new, makeshift bandage was unsanitary. If blood loss—or the man with the gun—didn't take her, surely infection would. She needed to get out of here.

Just because she couldn't hear him didn't mean he wasn't there. He might be messing with her again—or with himself. Revulsion triggered at the memory of the vile pink worm. It was the first time that she'd seen a man masturbate outside of pornography. It was the first penis that she had seen in person, period. How unfair that a violent man had gotten to choose the moment. It should have been her choice, but he had snatched it away from her, replacing what should have been a positive experience with a future boyfriend with a traumatic ordeal.

If only he had blown off the rest of her foot instead of her hand.

The thought was morbid, but at least she would have been able to move faster because she wouldn't have to drag the injured foot behind her. She was still in danger of losing her left foot, but she definitely didn't have a right hand anymore.

A fearsome vortex tore open—showering, eating, writing, cooking, tying shoelaces, making a bed, working a cash register—relearning how to live her entire life—but then, just as suddenly, it stoppered up. The protective act kept her focused on the current task.

Josie scooted forward on her butt. *Do it quickly.* Barely touching the lopsided boot, she released a ghastly cry. *Quickly.* The voice was stern. Hissing through clenched teeth, she grasped the injured foot and lowered it to the ground. A howl exploded out from her, screeching all the way up from her toes.

The night insects blinked, startled, and then resumed their trill.

If that fucker was still watching, he was relishing her pain more than ever. She felt like James Franco in *127 Hours* when he amputated his own hand after it got crushed underneath a boulder. But James Franco had been accused of sexual harassment, too. Was there any man left on the planet who wasn't a swine? She listed them to distract herself: Her brother. Her uncle. Neena's father. Neena's brother. Briskly, she inhaled and exhaled through her teeth, psyching herself up. With all her weight on her right side, she pushed herself up from the bottom of the sinkhole.

Josie stood.

Her right leg trembled and so did her heart. Grabbing the thick root that had snapped her ankle, she tried to pull herself out of the sinkhole with her left hand. Her right elbow dug into and scraped against the dirt wall, attempting to give lift. Her good foot scrabbled and pushed. Her efforts were as fruitless as they were monumental.

Depleted after mere seconds, she dropped back into the hole. Her swaying foot shuddered, the sinews ready to snap. She tried again and again, but each frenzied attempt was shorter than the last. Yelling, she cursed the man with every expletive and some that weren't words at all. Her frustrated gaze landed on the backpack. With the length of her bad arm resting against the wall for balance, her jawbone gritted, and she dragged the pack underneath the large root. She didn't know how she was dragging it one-handed. It had been almost impossible with two hands yesterday. *Super-fucking-human strength*, she thought, imagining adrenaline-fueled mothers lifting cars off their children.

She stepped on the pack, and this time when she reached upward, her hand touched the ground. But she still didn't have the strength to lift herself out with one hand—her weakest hand. Her good foot scrambled for additional leverage, but she fell back into the hole. Her bad foot cried out with an anguished wet pop.

Tears infuriated her eyes. She could touch freedom. She just couldn't get to it.

"I hope you're fucking happy," she screamed, before amending it. "Except I don't, because you're an asshole. And you're miserable, and you always will be, and that's your fucking problem, not mine!"

Her ears strained again, but the forest didn't give anything away. Where was he? What had he done to Neena? What would he do with her? She shrieked into the echoing night.

Preserve your energy, the voice said.

Josie was short of breath again. Her rash actions were undermining her efforts.

One thing at a time. Always do the most important thing first.

Grimacing, she twisted her body to root through her pack. The best that she could find was Win's Swiss Army knife. The longest blade was only three inches of feeble steel. She gripped the weapon with her remaining hand and awaited the man's return, her animal heart beating with vengeance.

NEENA

NEENA PICKED UP her headlamp and shone it onto the body. She covered her mouth in horror. A strong wind swept through the trees, and a gust of bodily odors assaulted her: oniony perspiration, blood like iron nails, the pungent stench of ammoniacal piss.

It was a young woman. She was splayed out on the forest floor, faceup and eyes open, wearing a long-sleeved button-down and nothing else. The shirt was undone. Her white skin was dirty and dehumanized, scraped with heinous scratches, obliterated with pounding bruises. Ragged red marks ringed her ankles and wrists. Her hair was plastered lankly to her neck, where brutalizing, fingerlike blotches still grasped her throat. She looked older than Neena and Josie but only by a few years. Maybe the age of their brothers. And she was dead. She *had* to be dead, but Neena also had to be sure.

She didn't whisper the words. She breathed them. "Are you okay?"

The young woman did not respond.

"Shit," Neena said quietly, crying as her voice rose. "Oh my God."

Bending over, her arm reached outward for inspection but then retracted. She forced the arm back out. With one trembling finger, she touched the skin. It was warm, barely. Though the muscles were still soft, it was clear that the person who had once lived inside this vessel was gone. Neena released a wretched moan. How long did it take for rigor mortis to set in? How long had this body—this *woman*—been dead?

She turned off her light, petrified, as her mind raced through possible scenarios: The man and woman were camping here together, and he'd murdered her. Or, this was the woman's campsite, and the man had stumbled across it, and then he'd murdered her. Or, maybe he had brought her here from someplace else as his captive. The two chairs and significant amount of equipment suggested they'd come here together willingly, but the only thing Neena knew for certain was that the man was responsible for this depravity. And she didn't doubt that he would return.

Total darkness eclipsed the campsite. Fear swallowed her. The flames had died, but the fire smoldered. Coils of acrid smoke wrapped around her throat in strangling, choking eddies. The eyes of the forest fixed on her again as she began to run.

JOSIE

HER STAMINA HAD succumbed, and Josie was back on her ass. Her bad foot was propped up on the pack. Goose bumps barbed her bare left arm. The damp sinkhole was cold and static, but her headlamp was at the ready, draped around her like a necklace.

The knife was still in her hand.

Another unforgiving object, hard and insistent, jabbed into the back of her thigh. When she mustered the energy, an oddly shaped pebble dislodged from the mud. Its surface was slippery-smooth. Tracing the C-shaped curve, she recognized it as a shard from her friendship ring. The shotgun blast had destroyed this, too. Had Neena made it out of the woods? Josie would give her bad foot to be in Neena's living room right now, snuggled together on the squashy couch and watching videos on their warm phones. She rubbed the sawtoothed edge before tucking the shard protectively into her pocket.

In a prolonged state of stress and fatigue, she drifted in and out of consciousness. Leaves shuffled in auditory hallucinations. Branches snapped. Once, she smelled his rancid breath. But whenever she startled awake with a fiercely pounding heart, it was always nothing.

• • •

Until it wasn't.

She didn't know when the man reappeared. It was the dead of night. In her mind, the hour was exactly halfway between sunset and sunrise.

The first twig was sharp, its dry crack unmistakable. It jolted her into alertness. The man walked straight toward her. No games. His stride was so purposeful that she knew some sort of decision had been made. She clambered onto her good foot. This time, she wouldn't greet him lying down. The small blade trembled in her clenched fist. The heavy footsteps stopped at the sinkhole's edge. Before she could make out his figure, a blinding light fractured against her crooked glasses and seared into her eyes.

"You're up," he said. A touch of surprise.

She squinted, refusing to block the light with her good arm. She brandished the knife like a sword.

"What's that?" He snorted. "You gonna stick me with a toothpick?"

Yes. And then she would drag his body down here and use it as another stepping-stone to get out.

"Put that down," he said.

"Come closer," she hissed.

In one fluid but unhurried motion, he tossed the flashlight to the ground and lifted the shotgun. His lower body revealed itself in ghostly, blurry form. The metal barrel winked in the light. Unlike the man, the barrel was sharply in focus, inches away from her forehead.

Ashamed, she dropped the knife. It landed with a dull thump. She felt young and frightened again. The gun had stripped away any last trace of bravery.

"It's time to join the others," he said.

Her heart constricted. "The others? Do you have Neena?"

He grunted and set down the gun.

"Where is she? What have you done with her?"

The man slithered onto his belly, and the smell of rotting teeth and diseased gums poured into the hole. She coughed and retched as he extended a meaty hand. Grime lined the creases of his skin. His fingernails were thick and ridged and plugged with dirty crescent moons. Maybe he was homeless. Or maybe these woods were his home. He seized one of her braids and yanked so hard that rooted follicles ripped from her scalp.

She made a sound between a gasp and a yell.

He let go and offered his hand again. "Take it."

Josie knew it was one of the golden rules of survival: Never go to a second location. Fight with everything you have from getting into a stranger's car, house, territory.

But this stranger had a gun. And she was powerless inside the hole.

The intensity of his voice changed very little. "Take it, or I'll blow you away right now."

He'd already proven that he would. "What are you gonna do to me?" Her left arm trembled as she reached up. "Where's Neena? Where are the others?"

"The others ain't alive anymore."

He grasped onto her with sandpapery hands and pulled. She screamed. Her good foot scrambled against the dirt wall for purchase, frantic to prevent her arm from being ripped from its socket. Her bad foot fizzed with bolts of lightning pain. Winded, he panted for breath, blasting her with the full brunt of his halitosis and the reek of her own dried urine as her body lifted over the edge. She rolled and toppled away. Her legs accidentally swept into his, and his footing slipped. Her eyes widened with the unforeseen opportunity.

Her good leg reared back like a horse. She kicked his buckling frame with purpose, and the man yelled in surprise as he toppled into the sinkhole.

Everything had happened so fast. Her senses reeled and stuttered. *The others ain't alive anymore.*

Her glasses were gone, lost in the transaction. Her gums were bleeding as she spit out the dried leaves from her mouth. She didn't know how they had gotten there. Missing a hand and deficient a foot, she had no chance of escape if he could climb out and follow her. He seemed tall enough and strong enough to be able to lift himself out.

She scanned for the gun and located it within reach. Belly down, she scooted and dragged herself into place, positioning the double-barreled shotgun against the ground at the edge of the hole. The stock was heavy and bulky and clumsy in her nondominant hand. Assuming he had reloaded, it contained two shots.

Grunting movements issued from below. A dark figure rose.

Josie pulled the front trigger. The shot was deafening, and she was no match for the recoil. Because she was unable to balance the gun against her body, it kicked straight back and jolted from her hand. Her eardrums rang in the furious silence.

Grabbing arms reached upward through the billowing clouds of dirt. The man was still upright and unharmed. She hustled the gun back into place. Channeling the training on her uncle's rural acres, she took a deep breath—just like he'd taught her—and exhaled as she squeezed the trigger.

It clicked. Nothing happened.

Panic fogged her. It appeared that the man hadn't reloaded, until her finger found the rear trigger. The shotgun kicked and blasted back out of her hand.

She scrabbled forward to peer down. It was too dark and dusty to see anything. His flashlight lay on the ground nearby, turned on and pointed at nothing. Its aluminum body was heavier than she'd expected as she picked it up and aimed the trembling beam.

This time, she hadn't missed. The man was sprawled at the bottom of the hole. Her pack was still under his feet as if he'd been standing on top of it when he'd been blown backward. It was impossible to tell where she'd hit him or how badly he was injured, but the mounded heap of his body was motionless.

Josie searched for something to throw at him, to test him. No other objects or stones were within reach, but her headlamp was still around her neck, and she would need the full use of her hand to get out of the woods. She threw the flashlight, hard. The tumbling light captured a flinch in his eyelids before making contact with a squelching thwack. The hit wasn't square, but it struck the side of his head. The white beam streamed upward into the sky. The light was unearthly, reminiscent of alien encounters and hostile spaceships. But the man was only human. And he wasn't moving.

She had no time to feel relief. She had no time to waste.

The effort to stand was tremendous, but adrenaline gave her strength, a staggering mixture of fear and euphoria. She collected the shotgun and tucked it underneath her left armpit as a crutch. Balancing and hopping and lurching away, the mangled foot dragged behind her. It bumped and popped across the earth as it caught on rocks and sticks, but she hardly felt the pain. Black spots kaleidoscoped her already hazy vision.

The others ain't alive anymore.

She fled from the light, back into darkness.

NEENA

SHE RAN UNTIL the campfire was a distant orange smudge. Her skull was swollen with shock. Terror pulsed through her bloodstream. Even without a closer look, she sensed that the woman had been tortured for a long time, perhaps days.

Dark terrain hurtled underfoot. Sweat soaked Neena's underwear, and her jeans chafed her thighs. The forest entangled her in a thicket of tendrils and saplings, prickles and briars. She cleaved through them in a splintering crash. Blackberry thorns zipped and stung her hands, snagged and tore her clothing, but she was already deep inside the brambles with no choice but to push through. Her lungs pumped, sucking the moist and bestial air. Gulping it. She wheezed in puffs that intensified into hacking coughs.

Her foot struck something hard, and she smashed to the ground.

The indifferent trees gazed down at her. The moon continued on its slow nightly path. Feeling for the object, she discovered a trifling nub of root. Tears spilled over her burning cheeks. She had run away without thinking, without a plan, and now she couldn't even hear the stream. She was lost. She had to find her bearings. The man was still out here, somewhere, hunting her. Hunting Josie.

Her mind thrummed with hectic calculations. Assuming that earlier he had been trying to lead her to his campsite, she could re-orient herself by coupling this information with the position of the westerly moving moon. It was only a guess, but a decent one.

She waited for her breath to regulate. When it was as good as it was going to get, she got back up. Her knees yowled in protest. Her thighs ached with stiffness. She turned on her headlamp but clutched the light to dampen it. Her glowing fist lit the way.

Steadily, Neena trekked northeast toward the Wade Harte. To have any hope of getting out, she needed to locate familiar territory. Fear churned her bowels as she slogged past the musty toadstools and stagnant pools, the dusky groves and pockets of absolute silence. Had she picked the wrong direction?

Unseen critters tussled with the fallen leaves. Bats swooped like startling apparitions. Every minuscule sound jackknifed her heart. Her ears were exhausted from listening so hard. Freezing and trau-matized, she shivered uncontrollably. Time plodded by, but, no matter how long or how far she traveled, she was always still in the woods.

Until—

A yellow-gold dome rose over the horizon. Elation swelled inside her as warm as daylight, but the beacon wasn't the sun. It was the tent they'd camped beside the previous night. No sight had ever filled her with such hope.

Opening her palm, Neena allowed the headlamp to fully illumi-nate her path. She scrambled up the slope and through the under-brush. Branches grabbed, but she no longer felt their claws. Rocks scraped, but she no longer felt their abrasions. She burst into the campsite and shone her light onto the tent. And then she gasped and staggered back.

A single, violating gash had lacerated the rear, creating a new door from the outside. The nylon had been split into two gaping flaps. The distressed fibers rippled in the breeze. Though the intrusion didn't appear to be recent, she spun in an anxious circle. But her shaking light revealed nothing more than the surrounding pines.

The hair rose on her neck.

This was the dead woman's tent. It had to be. If only she and Josie had inspected it more carefully that morning, none of this would have happened. They would have gone home and reported the crime, and Josie wouldn't have fallen into the hole. Neena wouldn't have been chased. The woman might even still be alive. The imprint of her screams from the moment when she had been wrenched from slumber and safety resonated throughout the mountains.

Uneasily, cautiously, Neena peered between the flaps. A hideous face leered back at her.

JOSIE

AS NEENA WAS still stumbling away from the first dead body, long before she found the second, Josie was staring at the woods ahead. They were as black as a cast-iron skillet. Propping her body against the closest tree, Josie wrestled the headlamp from around her neck, yanked it to her forehead, and turned it on. She did not look behind at the light issuing from the sinkhole. Squinting, she swept her lamp back and forth, back and forth—*there*.

She staggered toward a pair of bottle caps, untethered. Her face felt naked where her glasses used to sit. Her eyesight had smudged into a terrifying blur, but her other senses seemed heightened, sharpened, as if her pain sensors had shut off to provide strength for other operations. Had she killed the man? Injured him? She did not feel conflicted about having shot him. His actions had empowered her to protect herself.

The others ain't alive anymore.

He hadn't been talking about Neena. She couldn't let herself believe that. A great dam of grief quaked, threatening to crack and rupture.

There. Her desperate squint managed to locate the next pair of bottle caps.

Josie was traveling forward—not backward, the way Neena had gone—because she couldn't risk the additional time and mileage. She prayed the remainder of the blazes would be there. If even one blaze was missing, she was done for. Had the man pried off the bottle caps from the tree beside the sinkhole? It seemed plausible that he might have set a trap, but it didn't actually matter. Putting distance between herself and the man was all that mattered now. She hoped his wounds were severe enough to prevent him from giving chase, because otherwise her bloody, dragging trail would be easy to track.

She hobbled toward Frazier Mountain. Her injuries thumped hot. Blood weltered inside her shoes. Every step was an endurance test, a toddling balancing act between her good foot and the shotgun. The terrain was uneven, and her awkward grip on the gun was sweaty, tight, and strained. The stock dug an abusive trench into her armpit.

With agonizing slowness and feverish determination, the light from the sinkhole grew fainter. But even when it disappeared completely, she still saw it. Her heart pounded helter-skelter, deranged, and she was in danger of passing out.

She tripped over a bulging rock and smacked into the ground. Her bad foot screamed with the onslaught of pain. Gasping, tears flooding, she was unable to think. Several minutes passed before she recovered enough energy to push up against her remaining knuckles. With another cry, she struggled back into a standing position, purposefully not looking at her missing hand.

The gun crutch wobbled. Her chest spiked with the panic of falling again.

One step at a time, the voice said. *Just take it one step at a time.*

Was it the voice of the living or the dead—or something else entirely? From blaze to blaze, Josie clumped and tottered. The work was taxing, and she was at the mercy of the bottle caps. It wasn't clear which way was north or south or east or west. The forest isolated her in confused turmoil. Whenever she couldn't find a blaze, she shambled in dwindling circles, knowing this was the end. *This* was the dark place where she would bleed out and die. But then the blaze would manifest, and she would be saved.

The shotgun clinked, clinked, clinked with each step. Shivery and numb and delirious with tedium, she wished her bare arm had a sleeve. The mosquitos chewed her up. Her ligaments stiffened and groaned. A creek trickled a siren song, and her tongue bleated with thirst, but she knew the water wasn't safe to drink.

Not long after, she flagellated herself for passing it by.

She fell again.

The pain was blinding, starbursts and electric shocks. Immobile, she sagged into the limbs of a waxy-leaved bush. It was too difficult to carry on. Her chances of survival were too slim.

Except . . . Neena might also be injured and alone.

Josie's exhausted eyes peeled open, and her light shone a halo onto the next grouping of bottle caps. *One step at a time*, the voice reminded her. And she realized that it didn't matter who it belonged to. It loved her, and it would always be with her.

She picked herself back up. One blaze at a time, she continued through the woods, her bandaged foot bumping along behind her.

NEENA

NEENA REFLEXIVELY AVERTED her gaze before forcing it back to the decomposing man. His body lay supine with one arm bent outward at a warped and unnatural angle. Black flies and maggots teemed across stretched skin, which was marbled in bloated shades of gray and brown. Cloudy eyeballs protruded over a thickened tongue. The tent was ripe with the gassy stink of putrefaction.

Acid rose in her throat. She purged a mouthful of fluid bile, tasting the fetor of his rotting tissue. He had been deceased for much longer than the young woman.

We set up camp and slept beside a murdered man last night.

Her vision went white.

She blinked it, forced it, back into focus. The light of her headlamp exposed the cramped space. Dried pools of gunky blood. Gristly spatter, sprayed across everything—backpacks, sleeping bags, even the ceiling. The man himself was covered in so much that she couldn't even tell how he'd been slaughtered. The blood swallowed her beam.

Two backpacks, two sleeping bags. One body.

He looked to be about the same age as the woman. Beside an inflatable pillow there was a bra that looked as if it had been discarded before bed. *The man had been murdered so that his girlfriend could be abducted.* Neena saw the other man—the killer—wrap his sadistic hands around the woman's neck. With Neena's narrowed passageways, it felt as if he was choking her, too.

Overcome with an urgent need for water, she scrounged through a bloodied pack within reach. It was emptier than expected, and the haphazard mess within indicated that it had already been ransacked. She slipped an arm and foot inside the tent. Leaning toward the other pack, she dragged it over and discovered that its contents had also been dumped. She scoured the disarray until her lamp revealed a Hydro Flask that had rolled into a corner. The rest of her body entered the tent. Snatching up the bottle, she unscrewed the lid. Only about half a cup of water was left inside. She forced herself to drink slowly, but her hands shook so badly that some of the liquid sloshed out.

The corpse judged her endeavor in gory silence.

Sip. Her rib cage forced an inhalation and exhalation. *Sip.* Her muscles throbbed in agony. *Sip.* She repeated the effort until the water was gone. It was time to move again.

At least now she knew her location.

Neena plowed back out through the tent flaps. Psychosis engulfed her as the dead man chased her down the slope, pursuing her through the jagged darkness—arm crooked, elbow askew, fingers hooked. His figure morphed into the lean and rawboned killer.

She careened past the site where she and Josie had camped, disturbing the barrier of nightly fog. The pine trees disappeared into the vapors. Her boots crunched and bounced wildly against the spongy needles. She tore through the sagging curtain of vines out of Deep Fork and onto the Wade Harte.

She crashed into a halt. The trail was clear and exposed. Only now did it occur to her that the killer knew *exactly* where she was heading, because she had told him. He hadn't been chasing her through the woods all night. Most likely, he had returned to his campsite to eliminate the woman, and now he was waiting in the parking lot to finish the job with Neena. Or waiting somewhere else along this trail. It was easy to imagine him bursting out from the trees exactly as he'd done before.

There was another parking lot near Burnt Balsam, not far past their turnaround point. Despite their not seeing anybody yesterday at the overlook, it was the trail's busiest section. If she turned around and hiked back across the ridgeline, she was sure to run into somebody else eventually. It would take longer, but it would lead to help. She'd be safe.

But Josie would still be trapped.

And, because of Neena, the killer knew Josie's location. Maybe he wasn't waiting along this final stretch of trail, after all. Maybe he had gone to take care of Josie first. Maybe he was already there. The decision had to be made quickly. If Neena kept heading toward the Wade Harte trailhead, it was less safe for her. If she turned around for Burnt Balsam, it was less safe for Josie. The tunnel of mountain laurel loomed ahead—dark, descending, and ominous. The heavy leaves provided natural coverage to conceal and trap. Everything inside her shouted to run back toward Burnt Balsam and safety.

Neena chose Josie instead.

Girding herself, she headed toward the tunnel—as a second beam of light swept along the trail behind her.

Fear juddered her heart. She flicked off the headlamp and dashed behind the closest tree. Dirt clods and loose pebbles skittered down after her. Her lungs compressed tighter. Always, always, she couldn't breathe. With one hand cupped over her mouth, she tried to muffle the gasping wheeze. Her other hand gripped the fir tree for strength. The bark roughed her skin, but the branches smelled incongruously like Christmas.

The light was distant. The man was traveling slowly through the fog, but he was drawing near. Had he seen her? A mysterious, repetitive clink accompanied his form, similar to a prisoner being led in shackles. Each clink tolled a warning of danger.

Huffing one last time, Neena fell silent. The man was close now. Closer. Illuminated in the shimmering beam, a gun barrel struck the ground before her.

Terror exploded.

But the man kept walking. As his gun clinked away, the fog weakened into mist. In the receding light, she saw that the man's foot was dragging behind him. And then she saw that the man wasn't a man at all.

TOGETHER

THE WOODS WERE secretive. Trees older than death and saplings younger than spring watched over the creatures that slunk and scurried between them. The trees concealed. Shadowed. Obscured. Their trunks provided cover, their leaves bestowed shelter, and their limbs extended to make contact with fur and feathers, scales and skin. They knew everything that happened here, yet they did not take sides. They observed in silence. They offered these hiding places, but, predator or prey, it made no difference to them.

Neena burst out from behind a tree.

Josie shrieked and seesawed.

"It's me. It's me," Neena rasped as the same disbelief rushed through her—an unwillingness to believe it was actually Josie. Her best friend was nearly unrecognizable. Underneath the stark light of Josie's headlamp, her eyes were veined and bulging. Blood and dirt smeared her sallow skin. Bloody crusts rimmed her mouth and chin, streaked in vicious lines down her neck. She had one sleeve and one bare arm, and straw-like chunks of hair frazzled out from her braids and from underneath her hat. Her posture was stiff and broken, and, most alarmingly of all, she was grasping a gun like a bizarro crutch.

Josie floundered, lost to hyperventilating convulsions. Several fraught and raving seconds passed before recognition dawned in her eyes. Neena moved in for a sobbing embrace—and then discovered the missing right hand. She jerked back with a gasp. Josie's remaining sleeve had concealed the trauma. A crude bandage stumped her arm, and it was clear by the shortened length that the entire appendage below the wrist was gone.

"He shot it off." Josie sounded dazed. "There was a man."

Neena shuddered profoundly. "I know." In her mind, the man's helpful expression fell away as the gun swung in her direction. The woman lay dead and abused on the forest floor, the other man dead and bloated in his tent. Suddenly, she grew conscious of the brightness of Josie's headlamp. She lunged. "Turn it off!"

"It's okay," Josie said. "He fell into the hole."

This news stunned Neena. She dropped back again. "What?"

"He pulled me out, and I pushed him in. And then I shot him."

"*What?*"

Josie did not elaborate.

"Is . . . is he dead?" Neena asked.

"I don't know. But he wasn't moving when I left him."

Neena's breath hitched. The unexpected noise tuned Josie back into reality. With another wave of fear, she realized that Neena had been wheezing and keeping her words brief. Her skin was pallid, her lips dusky. They were both in critical condition.

"A man and a woman," Neena said. "I saw their bodies. He killed them."

The verb exploded like a bomb. Josie's ears rang. Her skin felt hot.

"Loaded?" Neena nodded toward the gun.

Josie shook her head. "I used both shots on him."

"How . . ." Neena couldn't finish the thought. She was staring at Josie in fresh amazement, and Josie understood this was a new question. *How did you get here so quickly? In your condition? How did you catch up with me?*

"The bottle-cap route," Josie explained. "Shorter. More direct."

They needed to move. Further discussion was unnecessary. Neena turned on her headlamp to double their light, and a murmur in the back of Josie's mind considered an argument about battery conservation. Just in case.

But the hell with that.

The girls began the excruciating climb down Frazier Mountain. They were severely compromised, so every downward step had become a potentially treacherous fall. Josie was still using the crutch, but now Neena was also providing support, gripping and lifting her up from the other side. It was a relief for Josie to lessen the weight on her armpit. The thin skin was rubbed raw and swollen, black and bleeding.

They entered the tunnel of laurel. The bushes confined, and the night tightened in. Together, however, their hope had strengthened. The parking lot felt closer, too.

A rifle cocked behind them.

Their chests seized. The girls turned around.

"Well, well, well." A man was framed at the top of the tunnel. "Look what we have here."

"You—you said you shot him," Neena stammered.

But this man was lean and wiry, and, even with her poor vision, Josie knew that she had never seen him before.

"I'VE BEEN LOOKING for *you* all night." The man seethed at Neena. His eyes were slits of rage. His muscles were as clenched as fists. "And look what I found instead. Two for the price of one."

Neena reeled with shock, which jostled Josie, who cried out in pain.

"I don't understand," Neena said.

"That's not the man," Josie gasped, her nerve endings throttled and whirling. "That's a different man."

The horrifying truth washed over them together. *Two for the price of one.*

The man inched over his rifle to aim it at Josie. "Now. I'm gonna need you to set down my friend's shotgun, nice and slow."

"I can't." Tears welled. Her good leg trembled. "I'll fall."

"I don't give a goddamned fuck if you fall."

Josie flinched and choked on a sob.

Fiercely, Neena held her grip. "I've got you."

Josie let go, helpless. The useless weapon clattered to the ground. It wasn't fair, she thought. Guns were *never* fair.

The man's rifle remained affixed to them as he moved to collect the shotgun, but the tension slackened from his muscles as soon as it was in his possession. Only the rifle had a strap, so he moved it onto his shoulder and carried the shotgun loosely in hand. Now that he held all the power, he didn't have to point it. Unhooking a flashlight from his belt, he shone it up and down the laurel tunnel until he located the desired swath. It looked the same as the rest. He held the branches aside with the full length of an arm.

"After you, ladies." The last word was witheringly simpered.

Josie curdled with revulsion.

Neena kept her grip firm as she adjusted herself to better support Josie. Her right arm wrapped around Josie's back. Josie's left arm and only hand wrapped around Neena's neck. Grappling with how to operate in tandem, the girls staggered toward the opening. Josie slipped, and Neena barely caught her in time.

The two halves of Josie's bad foot screamed with scissoring pain.

"*Move*," the man said. "I ain't got all night."

The girls hustled as best they could and ducked through the opening in the shrubs. A slight groove was worn into the forest floor on the other side, a pathway trodden by animals. Apparently, the men had been utilizing it for their own purposes.

The branches rustled back into place, closing like a door. Even with their three lights, the woods grew so much darker. The silence so much louder.

"Where are you taking us?" Josie asked as they stumbled forward.

Their abductor trailed behind them. Though his unhygienic stench reeked of violence, his manner distorted into something unsettlingly singsong. "Willie sure did a number on you. Hoo boy. You don't look so good, girl."

She raised her chin and hoped it carried into her voice. "My name is *Josie*."

"Well, Josie." Her defiance only seemed to tickle him further. "My name is Lyman. And I'm the last man you're ever gonna meet."

Josie's wounds pulsated inside their bandages. Lyman appeared to be a few years younger than the other man. He was taller and skinnier, and his features were all pinched together, while the other's had been wide-set. She couldn't smell his breath, but his body odor was worse. He was more talkative, too, although an erratic jitteriness undercut his relaxed demeanor. It seemed like an act, while the other man had been in full control.

"Where are you taking us?" Josie asked.

"Hey." He ignored the question for a second time, prodding Neena with the shotgun instead. An accusation. "You never gave me your name."

Neena knew *exactly* where they were headed. But since Lyman didn't know that she'd seen his campsite, she stayed quiet, trying to brainstorm any advantages this might give her. Concentrating was impossible. It was getting harder and harder to draw breath. Josie's unbalanced weight leaned into her, heavier than their packs. How much longer would Josie be able to survive without medical attention?

The muddy barrel pressed cold against her back. "I'm talking to you."

"You never asked for my name," Neena said.

"Well, I'm asking now. Like a gentleman. Which is more courtesy than you've given me. You know," he said, tone shifting to irritation, "fuck you. You're like my ex-wife, stirring the shit and then blaming me when the toilet clogs. Because of you, I've been chasing shadows all night. Because of you, Willie chewed my ass out. He's been blaming me for this whole goddamn mess like he had nothing to do with it. I *told* him he should have gotten you out of that hole straightaway, but he wanted to play."

Lyman was speaking to them individually, together, to himself, all at once. "Aw, man. I can't believe you fell for it. I told him it would work. I said if we covered that old sinkhole with branches— like one of them military booby traps—we'd catch us one. I can't wait to see the look on his face when I show up with both of you. Hey," he said, sharply interrupting his own stream. "How'd you get his gun?"

"I took it, and then I shot him," Josie said without emotion.

"Bullshit."

Josie didn't respond.

"So where is he, then?" he asked.

"Probably bleeding out inside the sinkhole," she said. "Or already dead."

"Bullshit. Bull*shit*," Lyman said, as if he was trying to convince himself. He probed her for more details, arguing with her and then denying her responses, growing increasingly worked up as they struggled through the forest. "He'll be there when we get back. He'll be there, you little liar."

They trekked for a long time yet still arrived sooner than Neena had anticipated. Perhaps because they had taken a shortcut. Or perhaps earlier she had only been traveling in circles. Perhaps she had never been far from this place. A dreadfully familiar glow lit the trees before them. The campfire was dim, but it was alive again.

Somebody was already here.

Lyman snatched the hood of her hoodie, holding her back. Neena lurched to a stop. Josie nearly fell beside her. Releasing his grip, he held up a silent, shushing finger, then waved the whole hand for them to turn off their lights.

All three went dark.

A flat clank issued from the shelter. Something metal hit something else metal, and moving shadows made scruffling noises. From the murky darkness of the campsite's edge, they watched a large and blundering creature emerge into the firelight.

"AW, SHIT!" LYMAN shoved the girls forward. "They told me you was dead, Willie." Getting a closer look at the injuries, he winced. "You *should* be dead, Willie."

Josie's tormentor was shirtless, although it took a moment for her to realize it. Willie was covered in an almost animalistic amount of hair, more like a grotesque coat of fur than regular body hair. The coarse curls were bloody and matted, caked with jellied gore around the areas where the shot had entered into his left shoulder and chest. He should have looked wounded and vulnerable. Instead, he looked dangerous and powerful.

She had shot him above his heart. Yet here he was, moving better than her and breathing easier than Neena, carrying a rucksack as though everything were normal. It made her question whether he was a man at all. Maybe he was something more. Something less. Something that could not be killed.

Willie was staring back at her, his eyes solid darkness as he slowly set down the bag. "You're still alive."

Josie's muscles went taut. "So are you."

Lyman held out the shotgun to Willie. "I told you I had every-thing under control." He sounded prideful and eager to show off his captures. "You remember Josie. And this one is"—his rangy frame snapped toward Neena—"hell, you still haven't said."

Neena screwed her mouth shut.

Willie grunted as he took the gun, the only indication that he was in any pain. Though he had the same accent as Lyman, his voice was deeper and measured. "Her name is Neena."

Neena startled against Josie, and Josie's shame reignited for hav-ing told him about her. Then again . . . Lyman had known about Josie. She and Neena had both been trapped in the same impossible posi-tion. This wasn't their fault. *None of this was their fault.*

The men were the only ones to blame.

Lyman glanced at the sack and then back up at Willie. "You were leaving?" He seemed hurt. "I told you I'd get her. I told you! Hell, I got both of them."

Willie ignored this, denying Lyman the praise he obviously wanted. "You'll have to dig it out." He gestured to his shoulder wound.

"Nuh-uh. No way. You need a hospital."

"No hospitals."

"Ugh." Lyman's nose wrinkled as his head turned aside. "Did you piss yourself?"

"Bitch threw it on me." Willie's voice tightened. Another indica-tion of pain.

Josie knew about pain. Her left foot was barely attached, her right hand had been blown off, and she had hobbled miles through the craggy darkness. Countless times she'd fallen, but she was still stand-ing up. For a moment, she felt triumphant. Pain meant Willie was human. But the reassurance vanished quickly. Because if she could still perform remarkable acts, then surely he could still perform un-speakable acts.

"Tend to the fire," Willie said, "then get this shit out."

It was an order, and he kept close watch over the girls as Lyman collected dry brush from a pile they couldn't see behind the shelter. The shelter wasn't big enough for the men to actually live out here, but the amount of work required to build it revealed that they had spent a lot of time at this campsite. This was a place they revisited.

The proximity of Willie's lecherous flesh was frightening. Lyman reappeared and hefted a large branch into the fire. The heat rose. Orange tongues licked at the night, revealing the ground to be littered with dozens of empty beer bottles. Firelight flickered and reflected on the brown glass like hazard warnings.

Neena trembled against Josie. Her gaze had locked onto something at the edge of the clearing. Josie craned her neck and felt the rest of her blood drain from her body. A long and misshapen lump was now visible underneath the dark boughs. It was a woman, dead and cast aside like another scrap of garbage. A portent of their own future.

Willie broke down his gun. The girls jumped at the noise, and the spent shells popped out, hitting the ground at Josie's feet beside a discarded bottle cap. She squinted down. Scarcely able to make it out, she was chilled to discover that the bottle cap was red with tiny white stars inside a blue X—Cataloochee Light. The same brand studding the trail that she and Neena had followed.

It didn't matter that they were inside a national forest. This forest belonged to *these* men. This was their territory. They hadn't just stumbled across her and Neena and made a split-second decision to abduct them. It hadn't even started with a chance encounter with the now-dead woman—or the man that Neena had found. Willie and Lyman had entered these woods with the explicit purpose of hunting for victims.

Lyman dropped another load of fuel into the fire. The flames hissed and sparked, startling Josie again, spiking her pain and making her cry out.

A depraved thrill rippled across Willie's face. An instinctive reaction of pleasure at her suffering. He dug into a pocket. Produced two new shells. Reloaded. His eyes remained fixed on her with feral intensity. The wind was cold, but he didn't seem to feel it. His body radiated heat. He was a predator, and he belonged in this forest.

He was going to shoot her.

But then he didn't. The distance between them closed in two heavy, steady steps. The full carnage of his injuries sharpened into focus. His repugnant breath made her stomach heave. With a feverish grimace, he grabbed her. His bulbous nose mashed into her cheek, and his sloppy lips opened against her recoiling mouth.

Josie tasted rotting gums, brown teeth, rancid tongue. She saw a ragged mother—angry from abuse, mean from alcohol and hard drugs—who liked to humiliate him. Called him names and made him watch when she was with her johns. He was filthy and unwashed and carried a bad odor. Kids bullied him. Teachers were repelled.

When he was six, his mother briefly married, claiming the man was his real father. He believed it back then, but he wasn't so sure now, even if they did share a name. William would take beatings from his wife, turn his rage inward, and then unleash it upon Willie. He once hit Willie in the head with the butt of a shotgun, the same one Willie carried to this day. Willie was knocked clean out for eleven hours before his mother's pimp drove him to the hospital. A dead kid would be bad for business.

Willie hated William because William was weak. But William's father—Willie's granddaddy—owned a tire shop, and, for a few good years, he took Willie out into the woods. Taught him how to drink and hunt. But when William was put away for armed robbery, Willie never saw him or his granddaddy again.

Willie's rap sheet for petty crimes grew rapidly. He did the seventh grade twice and dropped out in ninth. At least the food in juvie was warm. When he was sixteen, he raped a child in the neighborhood. She told on him—she'd said she wouldn't—and that got him sent to adult prison. They beat the shit out of him there, cracked his skull, and he vowed that he'd never get caught again. The girls would never again be alive to talk.

The full putrid sense of him overwhelmed Josie, which stunned her voluntary reactions into immobility. But one involuntary reaction remained. She vomited.

Fury threatened to burst Neena's lungs. "Get off her!" If she shoved Willie away, Josie would fall. She would never let Josie fall again. "Get off her!"

Lyman howled with laughter. "I told you, you gotta brush them nasty teeth."

Willie let go. His expression never changed, even as his hand wiped the puke off his face. But he grunted in brutal satisfaction. "Shut up and tie them," he said. With straining effort, he took a seat on one of the stumps that faced the fire.

Shock and sickness dribbled down Josie's chin.

"Josie?" Neena tried to say it gently, but her voice was too hoarse. She pulled the sleeve of her hoodie down over her hand and used it to swab Josie clean.

Lyman disappeared into the shelter. It emanated a menacing aura of masculine purpose, and Neena wondered how she had ever hoped it could belong to anyone else. The scattered equipment inside thunked and clanged as he rooted around, searching for something.

Glimpses of metal and glass and shiny plastic caught in the firelight. The materials gleamed as if the objects were new and expensive. Neena couldn't imagine either of these men being able to afford gear like this. Who had the camping equipment originally belonged to?

The ransacked yellow-gold tent. The footsteps in the fog.

Thunderstruck, she realized one of them had returned to the scene of their crime for a supply run. How many times had they done this? How many people had they murdered out here?

Lyman emerged with a length of polypropylene rope draped over a shoulder. He aimed the rifle at Neena's chest. "Over there." His head jerked toward a pair of trees behind the corpse.

Neena shivered but didn't budge.

Willie hocked and spit. The glob of phlegm landed on the toe of Lyman's right boot. "You never could make a bitch heel."

"Move," Lyman bellowed, in the natural transfer of human embarrassment: humiliation into anger into revenge on someone weaker. His rank body shoved between the girls, and he grabbed Josie from underneath the armpit of her good arm. The girls cried out as they were ripped away from each other.

His boot rammed into Neena, forcing her to stumble forward.

He dragged Josie. Leg scrabbling to keep up, she slid and fell. He hauled her across the ground. The pain was so extraordinary that she could no longer see or hear, only feel. She screamed, screeched, wailed. Lyman pushed her against a tree and then shoved her down into a sitting position, legs splayed out and arms at her sides. Using the hunting knife from the sheath on his belt, he cut the rope into two lengths and then held out the longer one to Neena.

"Wrap this around her, good and tight," he said.

Forced to obey, Neena wrapped it around and around, lashing Josie to the tree by her midsection. In Josie's condition, this was enough to secure her. Josie's screams weakened into gasps. And yet, through her pain, Josie sensed a purposeful slack in the binding. Somehow she held still enough so as not to give away the deception.

"Now." Lyman gestured with the rifle to the other tree. "Sit."

The second tree was younger and had less girth, so he was able to tie Neena's hands all the way behind her back, around the trunk. Picking up a third piece of rope that had been discarded nearby, he used it to bind her feet together in front of her.

He returned to Josie and tugged on the knot. His tongue clucked with reproach. "Well, that ain't gonna hold nobody."

Josie's hope shriveled. As Lyman began to unwork the binding, Neena released a macabre rasp. Josie understood that Neena's muscles were straining to exhale. The rope fell loose. Jolted by inspiration, Josie took a deep breath and expanded her rib cage as far as possible. Lyman tightened the binding. Josie held. He yanked and tightened. Josie quivered and held. Finally satisfied, he stood and picked up his rifle.

She exhaled, and the rope loosened—a titch.

He swaggered back around to gloat down at them. "My, my." His thin tongue licked his chapped lips. "Don't you two look pretty? Gonna have some fun with you."

"Stop fooling around," Willie yelled in a mushy garble.

Lyman's features screwed together like a child being berated by his father. He ironed them out quickly, aware of his spectators, but new wrinkles ironed themselves into the wrong places. The structure of his face turned demented. "Don't go nowhere, okay?" He barked twice with laughter—*what an original joke, what a comedian*—before striding away.

No doubt the rope around Neena's ankles had been previously used to bind the woman. Death had seeped into its strands. She felt it touching her, infecting her. She turned her head to look at Josie and rest against the tree. Dried blood in the bark, scratches in the trunk, and ruts in the earth further warned of a shared history with the dead woman. Her body was close, only a few feet away. Neena was close to Josie, too. If they weren't bound to immovable trees, they could have reached out and held hands.

"Are you okay?" she whispered, as Josie whispered, "Can you breathe?"

"Zip your lips, or I'll shoot one of you right now and make the other bury the body," Lyman hollered.

"It's in the—" Willie said.

"I know where it is." Lyman stormed past him and back into the shelter. He returned only a moment later, having fetched a small red box with a big white cross.

The first-aid kit infuriated Neena. They had no qualms about committing murder, yet they were still fearful of their own mortality. The corpse held a dark gravity that pulled her eyes again. Since she had last seen it, the body had entered into the stages of rigor mortis. The facial muscles appeared especially stiff and rigid, but no part of the body looked flexible anymore. Moonlight bounced off the bruised and battered skin. Neena wished that she could button up the woman's shirt to give her back some of her dignity.

Lyman took back Willie's shotgun and rested it out of the way, against the shelter. Then he set down his own gun at his feet before revealing a pair of tweezers.

Willie gave a derisive grunt. "You've gotta cut the shot out. An X over each one and *then* dig them out."

Lyman's brow furrowed, but he unsheathed his hunting knife. The huge blade glinted in the crackling light. He offered out a rectangular glass bottle—something stronger than beer—to Willie, who swigged and returned it. Lyman poured the liquor over the knife and then, with a wincing head shake, poured it over the open wounds.

Willie's scowl contorted into a huffing and lunatic grimace.

"You sure about this?" Lyman asked, handing the bottle back to Willie.

Willie swilled the remnants and then tossed the empty at the body. The bottle smacked the woman's thigh before thumping to the ground. Shining liquid droplets clung to his beard. "Just do it already."

Lyman's shoulders seemed to brace against an anticipated blow as he made the first incision. None came. His shoulders drooped with relief, and the surgery proceeded.

Slice, slice, dig.

The tools fumbled to reach each embedded shot. One by one, pellets dropped onto the forest floor. Sweat glistened on Lyman's forehead, and dark rivulets of fresh blood caught the light as they eked out pathways through Willie's chest hair.

Perhaps to maintain a tough appearance—or perhaps because he actually was that tough—Willie's cavernous gaze returned to the girls. "Morgan Shea Sullivan." His head inclined toward the body that lay between them. "Thought you should be introduced, since you're gonna have a lot in common."

Lyman chimed in. "That's what her driver's license said. We ain't stupid enough to take them, because that's evidence, but we always look."

"What was her boyfriend's name?" Though they came out in a croak, Neena's words were clear. "The man in the tent?"

Lyman snorted. "Now, that I couldn't tell you."

"Goddammit," Willie snarled as Lyman's hand slipped.

Cowed, Lyman finished digging out his current target. The shot dropped glumly to the ground with the others before his voice shored up with false bravado. "The guys are disposable, see. We ain't got no use for them."

The girls knew what *use* would come before their deaths. The taste of sick still contaminated Josie's mouth. It made her feel just as disposable.

Who was Morgan? Who *had* she been? Because of the similarities in their names and ages, Josie couldn't help but think of Win's girlfriend. Though new to backpacking, Meegan had taken to it enthusiastically. Josie had been angry to share her brother's attention, angry that it meant he spent even more time away from home. But Meegan had always been kind to Josie. She'd even encouraged Josie to join them.

Morgan's boyfriend was dead, too. Josie didn't know what Neena had seen, and she blocked out the gruesome possibilities. Imagining Win in his place was more than she could bear. Win and Meegan had always seemed so much older than her, but now she understood how young they actually were. They still had their whole lives ahead of them. Morgan and her boyfriend had none. Josie considered the boy with the deep voice and the girl with the milkmaid braid that they'd seen within their first hours on the trail, also so similar in age, and how close they'd come to being here instead. All of them walking through this same wilderness. All of it left to chance.

"How many?" Josie asked quietly. Just loud enough for them to hear.

Willie sneered. "We've been hunting these woods a long time. And we'll be here a long time after you're gone."

"Been here a long time," Lyman parroted.

"Others"—Willie winced as a pellet sludged from his skin—"they didn't tell nobody where they was going. Families and police think they're just missing persons. They don't know where to look."

"Our parents know where to look," Neena said. "They know exactly where we are."

Willie smirked. "But they don't know where you're *gonna* be. And it ain't here."

"Where?" Josie asked. The men were bragging and trying to frighten them. This was wholly unnecessary because she and Neena had been locked in a state of terror for hours. However, if they did manage to get out of these woods alive, Josie wanted to be able to tell the authorities where they could find the other victims.

She also wanted to keep the men distracted while her hand stretched for something inside her pocket.

Relishing his captive audience, Willie surprised her by answering the question. "There are other sinkholes. Caves. Places where a body can drop and never be found."

Josie flashed back to the bottom of the sinkhole. Rocks and soil and branches dumped heavily onto her body, burying her, gravediggers filling their grave. Desperately, her fingers fished for the object inside her jeans pocket. Maybe she was only imagining the slight pressure. Maybe it had fallen out.

"You hear about those murders up in Hot Springs?" Lyman asked.

Willie hissed and shoved Lyman away with his good arm.

"I'm helping, you damn jackass."

"Help better," Willie said, settling back again.

After a sullen interlude, Lyman continued, "That story was big. Three dead hikers and a missing boyfriend. We was worried that one got out of control, but the dumb cops"—he laughed, and the sound was tight and jittery like a rodent—"they blamed the boyfriend. He had a record—possession or some shit—so they pinned it on him. But he's dead, too. He gave us a chase, so we had to dump his body someplace else."

Willie's temper ruptured again. "Finish the damn job!"

Lyman flinched. His knife hand trembled as it hovered over Willie's chest. Maybe Willie was mad because they had revealed too much. Or maybe he was just mad with pain. Josie wished that Willie's pain would kill him. *Morgan, her boyfriend, the four hikers.* Six people were dead, although clearly they were claiming more. Josie imagined Lyman slipping again. The knife plunging into Willie's heart.

Her fingers clasped around the object. *Yes.*

"There were others, too," Lyman said, resuming his work. Slicing and excavating. He'd hardened himself back into a braggart. "Whores we doped up and brought into the woods. If you've been arrested enough, the police don't believe it when you actually go missing. Ain't nobody miss them. Fucking addicts."

"You ain't any better," Willie said.

"I'm better than them!"

Willie shook his head in disgust before addressing the girls. "First time we met in prison, he was on that shit. Been on it since he was born."

"Those women have family and friends," Neena said. "Everybody does. People who love them."

"My mama was a whore," Willie said. "Ain't nobody misses her."

The object slid out from Josie's pocket. The tiny shard of her friendship ring had broken flat on one end, but the other end was sharp and jagged. Wriggling her hand into position under the rope, Josie began to saw.

JOSIE HAD TO be careful. It couldn't look like her arm was moving. The twisted nylon frayed slowly, strand by strand, the beginnings of a faint fuzz. Fearing the tip might break, she couldn't push too hard.

Lyman was done. Or, at least, Willie was. After Lyman's hands were shoved away with finality, Lyman strapped on the gauze and bandages, sticking the white medical tape to Willie's woolly chest. It wasn't a good job. It couldn't be a good job.

But if Josie had lasted this long, Willie could last longer.

Lyman cleaned the blood off his knife. Willie groaned and stood up, vertebra by vertebra. When he reached full height, he was larger than he had been before. Staggering aside, he undid his pants. Piss streamed into the bushes.

Neena noticed Josie moving around, doing something with her hands. *Hand, singular.* Neena fought a nauseating wave of light-headedness. She owed it to Josie to stay strong. Josie, who was sawing. The action was suddenly, miraculously, recognizable.

How many hours were left until sunrise? It surpassed logic, but if they made it to sunrise, it felt like they could survive. These men weren't invincible; they were simply men. One wounded, both maybe intoxicated. Men made mistakes. What were their mistakes?

"I thought you were worried about evidence," Neena said.

The men, finishing up, turned toward her with perplexed expressions, as if they'd forgotten that girls could speak.

Neena sat up straighter against the tree. "Your DNA is all over that shot on the ground. You'll never be able to find every pellet in the dark."

The fire sputtered. Woodsmoke suffocated the air.

Willie slapped the back of Lyman's head, and Lyman skittered out of further reach. "Don't matter," Willie said, contradicting his act of violence. "Only my blood. Nobody else's."

"That first-aid kit looks new," Neena said, keeping their gaze fastened to her so they wouldn't look at Josie. "All of that equipment in there"—she coughed, smoke burning her impaired lungs, as she nodded toward the shelter—"is stolen. How is that different from taking a driver's license?"

Lyman crossed his arms. "That equipment is ours. Or it could belong to anybody. Or maybe we found it left behind after the murdering, and we didn't know no better, so we took it."

"All kinds of reasons why we have it," Willie said.

"The rope burns on Morgan," Neena said. "Those hikers at Hot Springs were bound in the exact same way."

"Yeah," Lyman said, "so they'll suspect the same missing boyfriend."

"No, they won't," Neena said, at the same time Willie expanded his chest and said, "Who says they'll find her body?"

"Why wouldn't they suspect the boyfriend?" Lyman asked.

Willie contorted with rage as he whirled on Lyman. "Why are you asking her? You think she knows something I don't?"

Lyman's hands twitched upward protectively, reflexively. As he lowered them, they clenched into fists. "I just want to know why she thinks that. In case we missed something."

"Stop trying to be smart, because you ain't." Willie lurched toward Lyman but stopped with another grimace of pain. "Just do as you're told, for once." Cradling his shoulder, Willie receded into the shelter. "Call me when you're done. And don't take too long." He gave a mean chuckle. "Then again, that's never been a problem for you."

Josie's sawing faltered. Halted.

Fear stabbed Neena—and then detonated into anger. "What, you guys don't like watching each other? *That's* where you draw the line?"

Lyman was stewing with fury, but this yanked his attention back to Neena. His posture righted itself. He made a show of sauntering over, his eyes glinting with the amusement of someone who knows more than the other person. "I like 'em alive." He paused for a terrible grin. "Willie likes 'em dead."

The words repulsed Neena to her core.

Harshly, Willie called out from the darkness. "It's your turn this time."

The smile collapsed on Lyman's face. A beat of silence blanketed the campsite. "Hey, man." Lyman swiveled toward the shelter. "I don't do that. That's your thing, not mine."

Willie exploded like a pressure cooker. "You fucked this up, so it's your goddamn turn!"

The silence following the outburst was deafening. Neena's terrified confusion over why they were still discussing turns upended, and her ears rang with the void of dread that opened around her. They weren't talking about rape anymore. They were debating who had the task of killing them.

Lyman's cockiness had vanished again. He looked deflated. Aggravated.

Lyman is afraid of Willie, Neena realized. Willie used threats and fear to control him, too. And even though Lyman seemed to be okay with murder, he didn't want to be the one who actually committed it. It was Willie. Willie had killed them all.

Neena glanced at Josie, trying to determine if her friend had reached this same conclusion. Josie was sawing frantically. Neena pivoted to a new tactic. Her heartbeat pounded through her skin, sweaty and palpitating, but her tone was calm and scornful. "Some friend, trying to drag you down with him."

Lyman's beady eyes narrowed even further. "What did you say?"

"He only wants you to kill us so that when you're caught"—he tried to argue, but Neena talked over him—"and you'll *definitely* be caught—you have no idea how hard my parents will look for you—you'll be held equally responsible for these crimes. That's a huge difference in sentencing, you know. Life versus capital punishment?"

Lyman hesitated, wariness muddling his forehead. But then he scoffed. "What the fuck do I care about your parents? Did it help the cops solve the case when the parents of those kids from Hot Springs boo-hooed all over the damn media?"

Neena imagined her own grief-stricken family on television, appealing for help in a press conference, all the distraught aunties and uncles of the local Bengali community supporting them in attendance. The clips would be recycled on crime blogs: Ma crying, supported in Darshan's arms, while Baba trembled bravely into the mic and pled for answers. Begged for anyone who might know something to come forward.

Neena's fear hardened into resolve. She and Josie would fight until the end. And if they went down, they would leave behind so much goddamn evidence that their families would get those answers.

These men would never have the opportunity to kill again. Improv wasn't Neena's greatest strength, but she gave it a go. "Okay, but even if you aren't worried about our parents . . . shouldn't you be worried about Galen's?"

Josie's sawing stumbled.

"Galen?" Lyman seemed to echo whatever Josie was thinking. "Who the fuck is Galen?"

Neena glanced at Josie. It was quick—quicker than the men's intellect—but loaded with meaning. "I mean, you said you didn't look at his license, but I thought that was a joke. You don't need an ID to know who that was."

"That guy in the tent?" Lyman asked.

"Galen *Cooper*?" Neena said. "Are you seriously telling me that you didn't recognize the governor's son?" Neena wasn't even positive if Roy Cooper was still the governor of North Carolina, and she sure as hell didn't know if he had a son named Galen. One of her loathsome coworkers had popped into her brain first.

"That's bullshit," Willie said, reemerging from the shelter. Neena had hoped that he'd already passed out. But not only was he conscious, he appeared to have heard every word.

"Yeah. You're just fucking with me," Lyman said to Neena. He glanced at Willie, but then his eyes bugged, and his hand flew to his forehead. His temper flashed again. "You're trying to play tricks with my mind."

"You guys killed the *governor's son*," Josie said, neatly picking up the thread. Though Neena doubted her own improvisational skills, she was wrong. The girls had had years of experience together. Josie understood exactly what Neena was doing, and she sensed Neena perk up as she went on. "You don't think the FBI will be all over you?"

"The CIA," Neena chimed in.

"The ATF," Josie said.

"The EPA."

Josie shot Neena a look, and Neena shrugged. The moment was so strange and off-kilter that they almost laughed. Thankfully, the men didn't catch it.

"They're messing with you," Willie said to Lyman, as Josie recommenced sawing. "Have your fun, and then shut them up for good."

Lyman was pacing. "I didn't kill nobody."

"No, you didn't." Neena's crosshairs locked on Lyman. "But do you think the feds will believe that? You need us. If you let us go, we'll tell them that you saved us. That Willie was the mastermind behind everything. If we turn on him, you might not have to go to prison at all."

Willie's muscles coiled and released, and he lunged like a snake, but Lyman reached her first. He was screaming as Neena's head smashed against the tree.

Lyman's scraggly fingers were gripped around her neck. Neena saw an addicted teenage mother who had given him up at birth. He was alone for the first three months of his life. His new mother, a Bible-thumping member of the Church of God, couldn't have children of her own. She was controlling, worrying, smothering. Always taking him to the doctor. The doc assured her that her son was fine, but she didn't believe him. Or the next doctor. Or the next.

His overworked father died from a ruptured stomach ulcer when Lyman was four. Lyman always wondered what his life would have been like if he'd had a father.

He made friends at school, but his mother chased them away. She chased away his girlfriends, too, so he married one of them at eighteen and moved out. Cayleigh was her own trainwreck, but she accused him of being insecure and immature and left him that same year. He went into the navy but was dishonorably discharged for sexual assault. While he was in prison, his mother—whom he both loathed and depended on—disowned him. When he got out, he was busted again several times for theft and possession.

Then he met Willie.

Willie had fantasies like he had. Willie had aspirations. Lyman felt lucky that Willie had even taken notice of him. Lyman would do anything for Willie.

"Stop!" Josie said. "Let go of her!"

Lyman released the stranglehold. His fingers transferred from Neena's throat onto his own, crawling up his neck like an infestation of spiders.

Willie shook his head in disgust at Lyman's failure to follow through.

"My father is a lawyer," Neena wheezed. "He can help you. *We* can help you."

Lyman was incoherent and unhinged, raging and cycling rapidly between emotions. Unbelievably, he appeared to be considering their bait.

"He's been calling you the fuckup this whole time," Josie said, "but he had me in a pit with no hand and no foot, and I got away. *You're* the one who captured us. He's the fuckup, not you." She was contradicting her own argument, praising him for being the one to catch them while also telling him that he was innocent, but Lyman didn't seem capable of catching the contradiction, so she pressed on. "We'll tell everybody that he's the murderer. That you kept us alive. Saved us."

"Willie will be sent to death row," Neena said, "and you'll be sent home."

The bark sloughed the skin off Josie's bare arm as she sawed, but the rope began to give way. It didn't matter how many times her ring had shattered; their friendship would always be powerful. Even the shards were strong.

"They're lying," Willie roared.

Lyman slapped his own head, trying to regain control of the chaos within. He was pacing again, agitated, unsure of what to do. Everyone was yelling at him.

Willie shoved him aside and lumbered toward the girls.

Maniacally, Josie sawed, bracing herself for the inevitable. Maybe she could stab Willie's injuries with the shard—or stab out an eyeball.

Willie's nostrils flared. He had noticed what her hand was doing.

"He was packing up to leave when we got here," Neena shouted at Lyman, pausing every few words for breath. "He was abandoning you! He thought we'd escaped, so he was leaving you behind with the bodies for the police to find."

Josie struggled against the weakened rope, trying to push through it with her torso. The shard slipped from her fingers. It dropped uselessly to the ground as Willie's eyes bore into hers with complete absorption, a pit that she could never escape.

His hands reached for her throat.

"You were leaving me!" Lyman yelled.

He barreled into Willie, pinning him to the ground, punches swinging in frenetic escalation. Though hampered by his injury, Willie was bigger than Lyman. He kicked up, dislodged the wiry man, and rolled on top of him. Almost as quickly, Willie grunted in shock. He fell back, palm pressed against his side as blood spilled out from a new wound.

Lyman's hand was clutched around his hunting knife. He was shaking—with sobs or laughter, the girls couldn't tell—as he crawled back on top of Willie.

"Push!" Neena said.

Josie strained against her ropes.

Snotty tears dropped down from Lyman's face onto Willie's. Willie's hand grabbed Lyman's wrist, blocking the knife, but he was expressionless as he forced the knife upward toward Lyman's throat. It was almost over. There was no doubt that if Willie won, the girls would not outlive Lyman by very long.

Lyman released a keening wail.

Willie huffed with steadfast determination.

Neena shouted at Josie to push.

Josie screamed as she burst through her bindings.

And then a fifth noise overtook them—a bustling of foliage and a powerful exhale—as an unseen beast thumped into a charge.

GIANT CLAWS TORE against the forest floor and whooshed through the firelit darkness. The bear was enormous. With an open jaw of gleaming teeth, it charged headlong at Willie, who released Lyman in shock. Willie's hands rose to protect his head. Lyman rolled away, scrambling onto all fours.

Time dilated.

The animal landed hard against Willie's chest, knocking him flat and pinning him down, tearing into his legs. Willie cried out. Snorting and snuffling, the bear let go for a better grip—to get a better angle with its jaws, those drooling white daggers of teeth—and then clamped back on, thrashing the body back and forth.

Lyman was shouting something, still crawling.

Josie sprang on her good foot toward Neena's wrists. Her teeth and hand tore at the binding as the bear backed its rump up against her. The bear felt *solid*. Its thickset muscles breathed and heaved. It smelled like a grassy wet dog that had rolled in pig shit, and, as she struggled not to be crushed, her fingers brushed its coarse and bristled fur. Willie was shrieking in abrupt bursts, but terror kept her muted as she clambered and tussled behind its haunches to free Neena.

"Shoot it!" Willie screamed.

Lyman lurched to his feet and grabbed the nearest weapon—Willie's shotgun, resting against the shelter.

The mauling was relentless, the biting and ripping. Willie flailed and punched, but the bear chomped down and tossed him as if he were a stuffed chew toy. Willie tried to scrabble away. A monstrous claw tugged him back.

Lyman swung the shotgun and aimed at the bear.

Behind the animal, Neena had a straight view down the barrel. It was still packed with mud from being used as a crutch. Lyman shouted as he fired. Neena braced herself, but the shot didn't blast outward. Mud trapped the shot, blowing it out the top of the barrel. The spray hit Lyman full in the face, and he keeled over backward.

Josie spit out the loosened knot.

The rope fell away from Neena's hands.

The girls darted away from the bear, both of them hopping, wide-eyed in manic disbelief. Neena's gaze snagged on the knife on the ground, near where Lyman had fallen, and she lunged. Blood gushed and pooled beneath him. Snatching up the knife, she sat down roughly to slice the bindings from her ankles. Lyman watched her, his face a surrealist nightmare. She couldn't tell if his eyes were open or closed, or if he even had eyes anymore. His body was unmoving.

Neena stood, and the rope dropped away from her feet. Still clutching the knife, she grabbed Lyman's rifle and slung it over her shoulder.

Scanning for Josie, the whites of Willie's eyes flashed at her through the chaos. A hulking paw was pressed into his back. The bear was winning.

"Shoot it," he said, struggling and huffing. A mutilated grimace tweaked his lips. His riven flesh was missing in chunks and hung in shining red peels.

"What about Morgan?" Josie asked. She was steadying herself against a nearby tree, berserk with fear. "We can't just leave her here."

"We aren't," Neena reassured her. "We'll tell everybody where to find her."

The bear growled and snorted with heavy, inspecting snuffs. It prodded the Willie-heap with its snout. Hot gore spilled out from punctured holes.

"Shoot it," Willie gasped, furious with desperation. His tortured limbs grasped uselessly for enough leverage to push the bear off his back.

Neena's arms wrapped around Josie.

The bear straddled Willie. His prone body was shredded and lacerated. The bear's colossal teeth ripped and thrashed. The ursine musk clung to the girls' nostrils, dominating over the iron-rich scent of blood—blood from the men who had believed themselves to be the most dangerous predators in these woods.

The beast roared, guttural and deafening. The entire forest shook. Neither girl looked back.

THE GIRLS HOBBLED through the forest to their escape. Behind them, the slashing tears and shaking thuds indicated that Willie was about to die. The sounds were reassuring.

"A bear," Neena said.

"I know," Josie said. "A fucking bear."

The girls exchanged a look, a silent pause to acknowledge the irony. But where had the bear come from? And why had it charged Willie and not them? Or Lyman?

The animal had seemed huge, but maybe it was actually starving because the berries had yet to ripen, and it wasn't getting enough food. Maybe it was a mother with cubs nearby. Maybe it had been attracted to the smell of Willie's urine. Or maybe it had even stumbled across Willie's scent trail and tracked him through the woods after Josie had smashed him with the mason jar. This last notion was the most satisfying. Though the girls knew it was incorrect to think of the bear as an ally—it could just as easily have attacked them— the bear was a force of nature, and nature had chosen to let them live tonight.

The clash grew fainter. Their ears rang numbly.

The girls traversed back the way they had arrived, retracing the worn pathway Lyman had led them down, praying the bear remained occupied. To conserve energy, they didn't speak. It was still dark, but they had managed to hang on to both of their headlamps, and, as they approached Frazier Mountain and stepped back onto the Wade Harte, they could feel how close they were to dawn. The nearness of the sun thrummed. The daytime insects had yet to awaken, but the nighttime insects were quieting. Birds chirped lethargically as the mist transformed into dew.

Their passage remained slow, the descent perilous. Loose rocks shifted underfoot, and smooth boulders were scattered with slippery grit. They fell many times. They had adrenaline, though, and they had each other.

They also had fear.

They could still feel the ferocity of the bear as it snarled and thrashed. They could still hear Willie as he grunted, bashing its muzzle with his fist. They passed the deer's rotting corpse. Although they couldn't see it, the fumes were harrowing. These smells and sounds of death resonated throughout their bones long after they left them behind.

Were the men actually dead? It seemed possible that Willie and Lyman might be supporting each other, teetering down this mountain, too. For the rest of their lives, the girls would have to keep looking over their shoulders. It was the reason why slain villains in horror movies popped back up, still alive—because there would always be another man waiting to cause harm. It would never end. The girls would never truly be safe.

Their bodies continued to deteriorate. From the exertion of assisting Josie, Neena's condition grew increasingly dire, but the car keys dug sharply into her ass, spurring her on. She wished that she could set down the rifle. It weighed too much.

She did not set down the rifle.

They labored in the correct direction but waited anxiously for landmarks to prove that they were close. These final extreme hours were like struggling through a time loop. Were they traveling backward? Was this even the right mountain? A stream tumbled over rocks, and Neena imagined her body gliding smoothly down the slope with the current.

Dawn broke, at last. The first pink rays shimmered with soft warmth, and the water illuminated. Directly ahead, the girls' cairn was revealed in the light of the stream.

They ground to a halt to take in the miraculous sight. Their stacked stones were still holding strong. Suddenly, Neena understood why she had fought so hard to leave them standing. The decorative cairn was a statue, a symbol, a declaration: she and Josie would always be there for each other. Whatever they had fought about—tormented by the grief of separation and fear of their unknown futures—it no longer mattered. Moving forward was the only way to survive. To live. And even though moving forward meant moving apart, it would be in distance only. Not in spirit or support or love.

The girls tightened their grips on one another.

They moved forward.

Time accelerated. Josie's foot felt as if it were already detached. The intensity of her pain had become meaningless, but each of Neena's sucking breaths portended to her last.

They passed the ancient oak. Two days ago, its singular crooked branch and knobby forefinger had been ominous, pointing them back in the direction they had come. Now it was a guidepost, ushering them safely home. The final stretch of trail was a fog of color and sound. Grassy green, mossy green, leafy green, dying green. Rasping, shuffling, coughing, scraping. They passed the brown national forest sign and noticeboard—and then three feet crunched into the gravel parking lot.

The sun had fully risen over the vehicles: Neena's Subaru, the other Subaru, and a pickup truck. The other Subaru seemed harmless and nondescript, but a menacing energy vibrated from the truck. Its chomping metal grill was massive and aggressive, the angle of its mud spatter violent and severe. It was indisputable which belonged to Morgan and her boyfriend and which belonged to Willie and Lyman.

"Walk me to the truck," Josie said.

Neena did.

Josie glanced between the gun and the knife. She was sick of guns.

Reading her mind, Neena handed her the knife. Josie jammed it in to its hilt. The back right tire released an exhausted squeak and slowly began to leak. Josie struggled, one-handed, to pull the knife back out. What if the men kept a spare underneath the truck's locked bed cover? Her plan had been to destroy all four tires, but the rubber had clasped immovably onto the blade.

Neena placed a trembling hand over Josie's. *Enough.*

Josie let go.

The girls managed the last few steps to Neena's car. Neena dug out her keys and swayed, taking Josie with her in a hard lean against the door. She was close to passing out. Every ounce of her remaining fortitude had gone into helping Josie reach this point. A life-threatening asthma attack was well underway.

This time, Josie moved to support Neena. She aided her to the passenger's side, unlocked it, and helped her into the seat. Josie hefted the rifle into the back. With her hand anchoring herself against the car, she hopped around to the driver's side and climbed in.

"Do you remember how to drive?" Neena asked in a faint gasp.

"I've got this," Josie said. Because she wasn't afraid anymore. The road was a blur, but she could see more clearly than she had in years.

With her left hand, she started the car. It roared instantly into life. Her left hand crossed all the way over her body to shift into reverse, and her right foot hit the pedal. The car obeyed. She shifted into drive as Neena plugged her phone into the charger. Josie stepped on the gas, and the girls sped away, waiting for a signal.

Waiting.

Waiting.

ACKNOWLEDGMENTS

AS WITH EVERYTHING I write, Kiersten White read more drafts of this novel than anybody else, and, therefore, must be thanked first. If we went into the woods together, I'm sure we could overcome any dangers that crossed our path. But let's not tempt fate.

Thank you to my fearless agent, Kate Testerman, who works with a machete strapped to her thigh and pom-poms in her hands.

Thank you to my brilliant editor, Julie Strauss-Gabel, who sawed this story apart and found a smarter way to put it back together. She does an infinite number of astonishing tasks behind the scenes and makes miracles happen.

Thank you to my badass publicist Vanessa DeJesús. Thanks to Lindsey Andrews and Sean Freeman for the marvelously eerie cover, and additional heartfelt thanks to Dana Spector and everyone at Penguin, including: James Akinaka, Anna Booth, Christina Colangelo, Rob Farren, Melissa Faulner, Alex Garber, Carmela Iaria, Bri Lockhart, Emily Romero, Janet Robbins Rosenberg, Kim Ryan, Shannon Spann, Felicity Vallence, and Natalie Vielkind.

Myra McEntire was my daily support team. Thank you for always answering your phone when it rings. Lauren Biehl, Manning Krull, Emily Maesar, Sandhya Menon, Kara Prahler, Heather Young, and Jeff Zentner also helped in tremendous ways with both story and research. Thank you, dear friends and dear sister.

My mother gifted me with her passion for books, but this one will be too scary for her to read. I'm thanking her anyway. And thank you to my father, who watched all the horror movies with me and popped all the popcorn.

Finally, to my husband, Jarrod: I'm sorry that I told you so many stories about bear attacks and serial killers before we went camping, but thank you for still dropping everything to go with me. Thank you for so many things. For all the things. There is no person with whom I would rather share a tent or house or planet. I love you the most, always.

"What'd you say? My connection is going in and out."

"So call me from the landline."

Haley glanced at the cordless, which was perched on an end table only a few feet away. Too much effort. "It's fine now," she lied.

Brooke circled the conversation back around to her current hardships as stage manager, and Haley allowed herself to drift away. She could only hear a third of Brooke's ranting, anyway. The rest was static.

She stared out the windows and finished her sandwich. The sun hung low on the horizon. It shone through the cornfields, making the brittle stalks appear soft and dull. Her father was still out there. Somewhere. This time of year, he didn't let a single ray go to waste. The world looked abandoned. It was the opposite of the loud, colorful, enthusiastic group of people she'd left behind at school. She should have stuck it out. She hated the quiet isolation that permeated her house. It was exhausting in its own way.

Haley made sympathetic noises into the phone—though she had no idea what she was sympathizing *with*—and stood. She walked her plate back to the kitchen, rinsed off the crumbs, and popped open the dishwasher.

The only thing inside it was a dirty butter knife.

Haley glanced at the sink, which was empty. A frown appeared between her brows. She put the plate into the dishwasher and shook her head.

"Even if we *can* get the sprayer working," Brooke was saying, their connection suddenly clear, "I'm not sure enough people will even *want* to sit in the first three rows. I mean, who goes to the theater to wear ponchos and get drenched in blood?"

Haley sensed that her friend needed vocal reassurance. "It's Halloween weekend. People will buy the tickets. They'll think it's fun." She took a step toward the stairs—toward her bedroom—and her sneaker connected with a small, hard object. It shot across the floor tiles, skidding and rattling and clattering and clanging, until it smacked into the bottom of the pantry.

It was the egg timer.

Haley's heart stopped. Just for a moment.

An uneasy prickling grew under her skin as she moved toward the pantry door, which one of her parents had left ajar. She pushed it closed with her fingertips and then picked up the timer, slowly. As if it were heavy. She could have sworn she'd set it on the countertop, but she must have dropped it to the floor along with her backpack.

". . . still listening?"

The voice barely reached her ears. "Sorry?"

"I asked if you were still listening to me."

"Sorry," Haley said again. She stared at the timer. "I must be more tired than I thought. I think I'm gonna crash until my mom gets home."

They hung up, and Haley shoved the phone into the front right pocket of her jeans. She placed the timer back on the countertop. The timer was smooth and white. Innocuous. Haley couldn't pinpoint *why*, exactly, but the damn thing unsettled her.

She trekked upstairs and went directly to bed, collapsing in a weary heap, kicking off her sneakers, too drained to unlace them. The phone jabbed at her hip. She pulled it from her pocket and slung it onto her nightstand. The setting sun pierced through her window at a perfect, irritating angle, and she winced and rolled over.

She fell asleep instantly.

●　　●　　●

Haley startled awake. Her heart was pounding, and the house was dark.

She exhaled—a long, unclenching, diaphragm-deep breath. And that was when her brain processed the noise. The noise that had woken her up.

Ticking.

Haley's blood chilled. She rolled over to face the nightstand. Her phone was gone, and in its place, right at eye level, was the egg timer.

It went off.

ABOUT THE AUTHOR

STEPHANIE PERKINS IS the *New York Times* and internationally bestselling author and anthology editor of multiple books, including *There's Someone Inside Your House*, *Anna and the French Kiss*, *Lola and the Boy Next Door*, and *Isla and the Happily Ever After*. She has always worked with books, first as a bookseller, then as a librarian, and now as a novelist. Stephanie lives in the mountains of North Carolina with her husband. Every room of their house is painted a different color of the rainbow.